STARMARK

To Charlie & Reuben,
Hope you enjoy
reading this!
        Katherine.

StarMark

KATHERINE HETZEL

Dragonfeather Books
Bedazzled Ink Publishing Company • Fairfield, California

© 2016 Katherine Hetzel

978-1-943837-02-1 paperback
978-1-943837-03-8 epub
978-1-943837-86-1 mobi

Cover Design
by

DESIGNS

Dragonfeather Books
a division of
Bedazzled Ink Publishing, LLC
Fairfield, California
http://www.bedazzledink.com

For Debi, the first person to believe both in Irvana's story, and in me as an author. Look what you started!

CONTENTS

ACKNOWLEDGEMENTS

StarMark has been a long time in the writing, a very long time. And I can't take all the credit for writing it—there are too many other folk who have helped me make it what it is today. I'd like to thank a few of them.

My Cloudie community and the friends I've made there—too numerous to mention by name—who have been constant encouragers and are more important to me than they will perhaps ever realise.

Debi, because she's a star! And without her, *StarMark* would still be languishing in the bottom of the wardrobe and I would still think I was a rubbish storyteller.

Jody Klaire, fellow Binkie on this side of the water, who has shared the publishing process, faith, and smiles with me.

Casey, for polishing this novel 'til it gleamed like a golden Mark.

The team at Bedazzled Ink, for publishing this story and for making it look so good.

And last, but certainly not least, my family. Nick, thank you for letting me follow my dream. And kids? I apologise for all the times dinner was late because "I've just got to finish this bit!" Love you.

CHAPTER 1
Changes

IRVANA HADN'T EXPECTED a frail old lady to weigh so much. But when she could barely walk and Irvana had to take most of her weight to get her outside, to see the stars before . . .

Irvana gritted her teeth, tightened her hold on Gramma's waist, and took another couple of steps. She wasn't going to think that thought. They were almost there, and Gramma would feel better for being out of the shack. She would. She had to.

"Here you go, Gramma. Sit here, against the rock. I'll wrap the quilt 'round. Look, we're just in time."

She could tell from the glimmer on the horizon that it would soon be dawn, but the brightest of the stars were thankfully still visible in the darkness above their heads. Otherwise it would have been so much effort, wasted.

"Irvana."

She looked quickly at Gramma. "What is it? Is the pain worse?"

"No worse than before." How faint Gramma's voice was. "Sit with me."

Irvana sat. In the darkness, she felt for Gramma's hand and gave it a squeeze.

"Ah, child, we've had such good times . . . not wanted for much . . . have we?"

It was a good job Gramma couldn't see Irvana's face. But just in case she could, Irvana shook her head and tried to smile. So what if her stomach rumbled sometimes and the driftwood shack that was their home wasn't always as dry inside as it could be?

"We've got each other. That's enough," she whispered.

Gramma managed a hoarse chuckle. "I remember the day you arrived . . . how long ago? Twelve years? You were tiny . . . mewling like a kitten . . . your poor ma dead not long after you arrived in the world and your pa drowned . . . just like my Freyd . . ."

"Don't think of that now. You know it always makes you sad."

The stars were paling in the rose light of a new day, winking out, one by one. Soon, there would be none left. Irvana loved to watch the dawn, when colours streaked the join between sky and sea. The sky was never blue as the sun approached, but pink and orange and green and purple.

"I've tried not . . . to dwell . . . on what I lost." Gramma's murmur was loud in the pre-dawn silence. "Too painful. You . . . helped ease the grief." From somewhere, she found the energy to squeeze Irvana's hand. "It won't be long . . . before I am lost too."

"You just need to rest." Irvana had to force the words out, past the fear which was threatening to choke her. "You'll soon be well again."

"We both know . . ." The old lady's breath was coming now in shallow gasps and she pressed her free hand to her chest.

"Gramma?" Irvana tried to will her young strength into her grandmother's body through their clasped hands.

"When I've gone . . . don't stay here . . . Go to Koltarn . . ." Gramma forced the words out between laboured breaths. "To the Broken Apple . . . Ask for Matteuw . . . He's the only one I can think of . . . who will help . . . Tell him . . . who you are . . . . Take my box . . ."

"Your box, Gramma? I don't understand."

Even as Irvana spoke, the old lady sighed a long sigh and fell silent.

"Gramma!"

No.

No!

Not yet! Another breath, please! Breathe, Gramma, breathe . . .

But Gramma didn't. There was no sound except the waves and the cry of a lonely gull. No breath.

Irvana stared at . . . at . . . at what had been a living, loving person moments before. Gramma was dead. Irvana dropped her cheek onto the hand that had relaxed so completely in her own and wept.

How could she carry on without Gramma? She needed her, needed her love and care. Life wasn't worth living without her. Irvana cried until there were no tears left and the sun had risen well into the sky. Then she raised her head and gazed through swollen eyes at the face of the woman who had been her only family for as long as she could remember. Gramma lay so peacefully, as though asleep, and she was still holding Gramma's hand. Her lifeless, cold hand. Irvana released a deep, shuddering sigh and tucked Gramma's hand inside the quilt.

Then, stiff and numb after so long sitting on the floor, Irvana got up. Her legs moved automatically, taking her to the edge of the cliff, where she felt the warm breeze caress her skin. She could smell the salty tang of the sea, even up here. Everything was the same—the sun still shone, the sea still washed the pebbles, the birds still soared above the water— and yet everything was different.

Irvana wrapped her arms around herself and held tight. It shouldn't be like this. The world should have stopped spinning. A light wind played with her hair, teasing it loose from its plait, as though by tickling her cheek it could put a smile back onto her face.

Not a chance. Irvana felt like she might never smile again.

She turned her back on the sea and the sun. She had to keep her mind occupied. She had to do something with Gramma's body.

There was a possibility that niggled at her from one of Gramma's stories. Fire! That was it. That was how the city folk sent the spirits of the dead on their way to the next life: in the smoke. Was that something she could do? The shack was wood after all and there was a little fish oil left to burn . . . But that meant destroying the place she'd called home, and she wasn't prepared to do that.

You won't need the shack if you go to the city, a treacherous little voice whispered in her head, but Irvana ignored it. She wasn't going to think about what Gramma had said. Not yet. She needed to deal with what was left of Gramma first.

If she wasn't going to use fire, what other options were there?

A hole in the ground? Gramma used to bury the fish bones so the wolves and bears wouldn't smell them and come out of the forest. The soil at the top of the cliff was stony, true, but it might still be possible. And if she dug close to the rock where Gramma had died, she wouldn't have to move the body very far either . . .

A sharp stone served as a crude spade and Irvana scraped at the soil until the sun was high over her head. That's when she stopped and flung the stone away.

"It's no use! It's too hard."

Tears and sweat stung her eyes. She'd dug all morning, and only managed to make a shallow dent, nowhere near deep enough to do the job it needed to. It made her feel sick, the thought that she'd failed and would have to leave Gramma where she was, propped up against the rock.

Irvana wouldn't let that happen. She sat back on her heels and forced herself to think. There had to be something.

What about stones? Brought up from the beach and piled around the body? It wouldn't be easy, and wasn't the best solution, but . . .

Using the quilt, Irvana tugged and pulled until Gramma's body was lying in the depression she'd scraped. Then she pulled the quilt over the face she would never see smile again and began the next part of her plan.

Irvana trekked up and down the crooked path between the stony cove and the shack at the top of the cliff many times. She carried the stones in a coarse woven basket and heaped them first around the sides of the body, then stacked them as closely as she could on top. The sun was beginning a lazy descent towards the sea again before she finished and added a line of shells along the length of the cairn, but eventually she stopped, satisfied she'd done enough.

With a groan, she stretched her aching arms and dragged her feet back to the shack. She really ought to eat.

It felt empty inside, even though there were still two beds, a shelf of pots and pans, a rough table with its crooked stools tucked underneath. Irvana went through the motions of eating and drinking, but didn't taste a thing. She was tired, but now that the physical work was done, her brain took over and reminded her of what Gramma had said.

Gramma had told her to leave, to go to the city—but this was Irvana's home. She knew this place; knew the single-roomed shack where all was neat and tidy inside just as Gramma liked it, knew the forest behind and the stream which skirted their homestead before running over the cliff and into the sea in the little cove below. She knew how to catch fish and how to harvest roots and fruit. She even knew where she could trade fish for flour on the roads through the forest. She knew enough to be able to look after herself, even if that meant denying Gramma's dying wish.

But would Gramma haunt her if she didn't go?

Irvana bit her lip, climbed into bed, and pulled her quilt up under her chin. Why would Gramma send her to Koltarn? She had never shown any sign of wanting to go back, in spite of all the stories she told about her old life there. The city had seemed to hold too many painful memories.

A shiver ran down Irvana's back as she slipped into an exhausted sleep.

CHAPTER 2
Gramma's Box

THE FIRST THING Irvana did on waking was roll over to smile at Gramma.

"Morning, Gram—"

The bed was empty.

Irvana choked back a sob. She'd dreamed it all, hadn't she? But the stiffness in her shoulders and arms and the yawning space where Gramma should have been told her otherwise. So she got up and broke her fast, trying to fill the emptiness with food. But she couldn't put off what she knew she had to do.

She had to decide. To stay, or to go?

It was a hard life here, on the coast. Especially when the winter storms raged and the wind whistled between the gaps in the driftwood walls. There had been times when there hadn't been enough to eat, when wolves had circled the shack, when sickness had meant being unable to fish or forage. But before, there had always been two of them . . .

Of course, it might be just as difficult to live in the city, even assuming that Irvana could get there. She'd have to avoid the bandits and wild animals who'd made the forest their home first. Come to think of it, Gramma had never said anything bad about the city—there were jobs there, and plenty of food.

And there was this man Gramma had spoken of, Matteuw. Who was he? If he was willing to help Irvana, moving to the city might not be so bad. Had he known her parents, she wondered. Gramma had never told her much about them.

Perhaps there was something in Gramma's box to help explain.

On the shelf above the table was the small wooden casket

which had sat there for as long as Irvana could remember. She took it down and stroked its lid, tracing the outlines of the flowers carved into its surface. She had never been allowed to touch Gramma's box. The long-dead Freyd had made it himself and it had been considered too precious for a child's fingers even though it wasn't a delicate piece of workmanship, being rather thick based and crude in design. Whenever Irvana had begged to be allowed to look inside, Gramma had always replied, "When you're older." Well, right now, Irvana felt much, much older than her twelve years—and there was no one to tell her she couldn't.

She put the box on the table, took a deep breath, and opened the lid.

There wasn't much inside.

A handful of shells, similar to the ones she'd laid along Gramma's last resting place, their iridescent insides gleaming. A tarnished silver pendant, shaped like an apple, on a broken chain. Hadn't the tavern been called the Broken Apple? A gold signet ring set with a scratched blue stone which she tried on, but it was far too big and slipped off her finger. Perhaps it had been Freyd's. A handkerchief, edged with delicate lace and yellowed with age. A lock of white hair, tied with a black ribbon—but whose head had it been cut from? And a single flower, faded and grey, which crumbled as Irvana stroked the petals, releasing the ghost of their scent.

Tears of disappointment filled Irvana's eyes. There was nothing here to help her. Everything must have meant something to Gramma, but it was too late to find out what. The tears spilled over and ran down Irvana's cheeks, shed, not just for her grandmother but for the stories represented by the objects which had never been told.

Eventually she wiped her eyes dry. Decision time. Was she willing to risk everything and go searching . . . for what? Information about her parents? A new future in the city? Was she brave enough? Yes, especially if Matteuw helped.

And just like that, the decision was made.

There seemed little sense in waiting. It didn't take long to collect everything she needed: the cleanest and least patched clothes, a good thick cloak, and some dried fish and flatbread. Gramma had said to take the box so Irvana closed the lid and added it to the rest of her possessions, wrapping everything in her cloak. Then she picked up her bundle and walked out of the shack, closing the door behind her.

"Sleep well, Gramma," she whispered to the rocky pile and walked into the forest.

CHAPTER 3
Helping Hands

THE SUN MUST have risen high in the sky, but the forest floor remained gloomy and cool, forcing Irvana to walk quickly to keep warm. She walked until her stomach started to rumble, telling her it must be lunchtime, so she stopped to eat at a place she recognised, where the trees were scored through by a deeply rutted track. The last time she'd been here was a full year ago. She'd been with Gramma then, trading dried fish with the folks travelling to the annual city fair.

Now, Irvana was very much on her own. Her eyes prickled, but she refused to let herself cry. Weeping would do no good now. Instead, she squared her shoulders, hefted her bundle higher, and stepped out onto the rough road, heading south.

As she trudged along her route, she felt like she was the only person in the forest. Even so, she kept alert, watching and listening for any sign that might indicate danger. The sound of a vehicle, approaching from behind, made Irvana's heart leap in her chest. Was it bandits? Panting with fear, she scrambled off the track and pressed her body close to a tree trunk, concealing herself as best she could.

The cart which rumbled into view was a simple affair, little more than a box on wheels, pulled by a plodding grey horse. It was being driven by a young man who was grinning at the woman sitting beside him.

Irvana could see nothing to fear here; these folk looked too ordinary. As the cart drew closer, she stepped out from her hiding place and moved to the edge of the track. The woman must have caught sight of her, because she dug her elbow into the man's ribs. He pulled hard on the reins and the cart drew to a halt.

"What's this, Matild?" he said. "Surely 'tis not one of the woodland fairies?"

Irvana craned her neck to look up into two curious faces.

"Whatever are you doing in the forest, child? It's miles to the nearest homestead." Matild squinted and pursed her lips. "Are you lost?"

Irvana shook her head. Her insides were quivering. How much should she tell these strangers of her plans? She knew she must look odd, and hoped, too late, that there were no leaves caught in her dark hair or dirt on her face.

"I'm going to the city," she said, hugging her bundle of possessions close, like a shield.

"There's a long way to go yet, child. Your family are happy with you travelling alone so far?"

Irvana looked down at the ground. She would start to cry if she carried on looking at Matild's concerned face. Instead, she concentrated hard on watching the beetle scuttling across the toe of her boot. "I've no family left. My Gramma told me, just before she . . . She told me to find the Broken Apple in Koltarn and a man she used to know. He'll help me."

When silence greeted her words, Irvana looked up and saw the carter and Matild exchange a glance. The man gave an almost imperceptible nod.

Matild flashed him a quick smile. "Well, then, 'tis your lucky day. We are heading to the city ourselves. I know for a fact that Simean here will be able to tell you the whereabouts of the Broken Apple, because he seems to be familiar with the location of most of the taverns in Koltarn. Would you be happy to ride onward with us?"

Relief turned Irvana's knees to jelly. "Oh! I would. Thank you."

Simean jumped down and helped her climb into the back of the cart, then rearranged the baskets of fruit and vegetables to make room for her. "Comfy?" He waited until Irvana nodded, then climbed back onto the driving box, cracked the reins across the back of the horse, and the cart rumbled onwards.

"I can't thank you enough for this," Irvana said a little later, as the miles were eaten up under the wheels. "My feet were starting to ache. I hadn't realised the city was so far away."

Simean chuckled. "Aye, and it's a good distance yet. You'd best rest while you can. What's your name, child?"

"Irvana."

"Well, Irvana, you'll need to do a fair bit more walking in the city, though I'll take you as close to the Broken Apple as I'm able in the cart."

"Have you been to Koltarn afore?" Matild asked over her shoulder.

"Never. Gramma talked about it though."

"Well, it's a grand place, though we only go there once a year."

Irvana felt an unexpected surge of excitement and fired a string of questions at Matild. "Once a year? Is it time for the great fair? Is that why you're going? What's it like?"

Matild laughed and shifted on her seat so that she could speak to Irvana more easily. "Aye, it's the great summer fair. A chance for us to sell our extra produce and trade for goods we can't grow. It's a huge event, brings visitors from all over."

"Tell me about it, please." Irvana had heard all about it from Gramma, but she was quite content to hear about it again.

"Rich folk live there in the summer," Matild told her, "cos the city is on the coast, see? It clings to the cliff and is far cooler at this time of year than further inland. It's also time for the hiring, so there's many who come in search of work." She paused. "Then, of course, there are those who visit purely to show themselves off and be entertained."

Simean laughed. "You're jealous, lass. I think you'd quite

like to live it up like some of those fancy painted ladies. And of course, there's always one who makes his presence felt in the summer. He's bound to be there, I'd bet my baskets on it."

"I wonder what scandals will follow him this time?" Matild said.

"The usual. Wine and women, I should think."

Irvana's curiosity was roused. "Who are you talking about?"

Matild frowned and crossed her arms. "Terenz."

"Who?"

"Lord Terenz. If I had impressionable sons or daughters, I'd lock them up over the summer for fear of his influence. The things he gets up to—"

Simean gave a great bellow of laughter. "Terenz is a man, Matild, and he's not yet wed. Let him have his fun, for it soon stops when one good woman takes a fancy to you." So saying, he hugged Matild to his side and landed a great wet kiss on her cheek.

Matild scowled and slapped him, but a smile played over her mouth and there was a twinkle in her eye. "You'd be lost without me, Simean, you great lump."

He grinned and turned his attention back to the driving. There were more carts and people now as several of the smaller tracks converged to form one, much wider, road. Everyone was travelling in the same direction: south.

"Tell me more about Lord Terenz," Irvana begged.

"He's Koltarn's overlord, answers to the Council in Bernea," Simean said.

"He isn't often seen by the likes of us," Matild added. "But I've heard tell from those who've crossed his path that he is tall, dark, and handsome, with eyes like metal, hard and cold."

"I've heard tales . . ." Simean began.

Matild gave him a warning glance.

"Not long now . . . See, up ahead?" Simean lifted his chin and nodded.

Irvana gripped the sides of the jolting cart and forgot all

about Lord Terenz as she leaned round Matild. The trees were thinning, the green gloom of the forest giving way to dappled sunlight, until suddenly the trees were behind them and they were in bright sunlight. She squinted in the glare and gazed in wonder at what lay ahead.

The road wound from the forest edge and down, through fields of swaying corn, towards the foot of an imposing cliff. At the base of the cliff was the city, its fortified walls wrapped tight around what had to be hundreds of buildings. The houses clung to a steep slope, which swept up from a busy harbour to the point where the cliff started and it became too sheer for anything to be built on it. The natural fortress the cliff created was topped with walls of pale gleaming stone.

So that was Koltarn. A shiver ran through Irvana's body. Was it fear or excitement? She couldn't tell.

Simean drove onwards through ever-thickening crowds. The road levelled out as they drew closer and stretched far away on either side of it was the city wall. It seemed to grow taller the closer they got—Irvana had to crane her neck to see the top of it. The cart was forced to slow to walking pace as the road narrowed on the final approach and the mass of people and vehicles squeezed together to pass through the gate. How Simean avoided running over any of the people travelling on foot, Irvana could not imagine—several of them were pressed dangerously close to the cart's wheels.

She caught a brief glimpse of a rusty portcullis above her head, then the cart rumbled on into echoing darkness as it moved through a wide passageway cut into the thick walls. Then they were out the other side, and inside the city.

"There's no sky here," Irvana whispered.

The buildings were clustered so tightly together, only thin slivers of daylight reached the cobbles and the cart. Trapped among the bricks and timbers, Irvana fought the sudden urge to jump out of the cart and run back the way she'd come until there were open heavens above her head again.

And the smell!

It wasn't fresh sea air, that's for certain. She gagged at the stench and covered her nose with her hand, trying not to breathe too deeply. It was even worse than the time when winter storms had washed a dead shark into the cove below the shack. The shark had lain there, rotting, until the next high tide washed the corpse out to sea. The smell of the city was a mixture of people and animals and sewage, all of it trapped in the tight cobbled streets. Occasionally, Irvana breathed in the more welcome aroma of food—meat and pastry—but that only made her stomach growl with hunger and added to her nausea.

How could so many people live in one place? And all of them so different. Some were richly dressed in silks and velvet, the ladies in dresses whose eye-catching colours reminded Irvana of the shoals of fish that used to dart among the rock pools. These lucky few were attended by servants, who carried boxes and bags or cleared a route through the crowds by hitting with short sticks anyone who got in their way.

Often on the receiving end of the blows were working folk, dressed simply in wool or leather, carrying the tools of their trades or goods for sale. The sight of an elderly woman, her face weathered with age, stooped low under the weight of a basketful of fish strapped to her back, sent a fresh stab of pain through Irvana's heart.

"Spare a mite, for my 'ungry babe, miss!" A dishevelled woman, clutching a sickly looking child to her chest, ran beside the cart and thrust a dirty hand under Irvana's nose.

"Oh!" Irvana fell back, startled.

"Get on with you!" Matild slapped the hand away, grabbed a couple of apples from the nearest basket, and tossed them towards the woman.

The woman bent to snatch the fruit up, only to have it whisked from under her nose by a grubby child. Boy or girl? It was impossible to tell under the layers of dirt. The curses of the woman were soon lost in the distance as Simean drove the cart on.

Irvana shuddered.

"There's many beggars in the city," Simean said. "I don't begrudge a little of the contents of my baskets, if it keeps them from stealing my purse."

The cart continued its slow progress through winding streets lined with houses three or four floors high. Simean manoeuvred expertly around tight corners and skimmed past oncoming vehicles and people until finally, the street opened out onto a wide paved square.

Irvana's jaw dropped. Decorated buildings hemmed them in on all sides. The cliff rose high above them, a great chunk of stone and beneath it, the entire population of the city seemed to have gathered for the fair.

At least the air was fresher here. Irvana took a deep breath, filling her lungs and clearing her nose of the stink of the streets.

"We'll be lucky to find a spot that's not in the alleys," Simean muttered, scanning the mass of people and carts whilst urging the horse forward. With some considerable effort, he nudged the cart into a gap near the centre of the square and threw the reins over the horse's back. He jumped down and hailed the carters on either side before helping Matild to alight. "I'll take the girl to the Apple," he told her.

Irvana didn't wait to be helped—she jumped down from the cart and grabbed her bundle.

Matild wagged her finger at Simean. "Don't you think of spending any coins at the Broken Apple before we've earned them. You drop Irvana off and come straight back here. Without wetting your whistle."

Simean grinned sheepishly. "As if I would. Come, Irvana, the tavern's not far away."

"Take care," Matild called, and turned away to serve her first customer.

Simean took Irvana's elbow and steered her into the crowd. At first she kept close to him, afraid of the folk who jostled and bumped her as they went about their business.

But she soon forgot her unease at the sight of what was being offered for sale.

How could Simean walk straight past the cart filled with sweet-smelling strawberries, all of them far bigger than the tiny fruits Irvana had grown back at the shack? And what was that strange-looking thing on the same stall? Like a huge stripy green ball. One had been split open, showing an inside of bright red flesh dotted with black seeds. And look at those blankets—every colour under the sun, and warm too, by the look of it. She smelt the fish before she saw them, their silver scales glinting in the sun, and marvelled at the strange contraption a man was using to sharpen knives. How did that work?

Then there was a space with no more carts or stalls. An area had been roped off and was filled instead with a wide assortment of people.

"What's this?" Irvana said.

"This is the hiring stand," Simean told her. "You stand here if you're wanting work."

What kind of work? Irvana studied some of those standing near the edge of the roped area. There was a man, his ink-stained fingers clutching a bag stuffed full of quills and parchment. A little further away, a group of burly men leaned on shovels and pickaxes, chatting easily. A young woman perched on the end of a wooden trunk, her fingers adding coloured stitches to a shirt, no doubt preparing it to join the other finely embroidered pieces displayed by her side. There were children too, some as young as five or six years of age.

A man, covered head to toe in black soot, grabbed the arm of a small boy and tore him away from a woman's side. Money exchanged hands and the woman hurried away, her face twisted and hands pressed over her ears, blocking out the cries of the child she'd left behind.

"They sell children here?" Irvana whispered.

Simean looked sad as the boy was dragged out of the rope

boundary, still calling for his mother. "Some do, if they've too many mouths to feed. At least it's better than begging. This way, the boy has a trade, though that of the sweep is a hard one."

If she couldn't find Matteuw, would she be reduced to selling herself for a trade? Irvana wondered.

"The Broken Apple is just along there, see?" Simean pointed to a three-storey building at the edge of the market place.

A crooked timber frame was dark against whitewashed walls, and mullioned windows looked over the busyness below. Above the door, hanging from an iron hook, was a brightly painted sign showing a rosy apple split in two by a silver cleaver.

"I'd best leave you here. I'll not let Matild say I was tempted by the apple wine this early in the day." Simean patted Irvana's arm.

She supposed he thought the gesture would reassure her, but she could see the unease on his face. "Thank you," she said anyway.

With a final pat on her arm, Simean walked away.

Irvana watched until the crowds swallowed him up, and then turned her attention to the tavern, trying to ignore that her stomach was performing flip flops and her mouth was uncomfortably dry. This was where she'd find Matteuw. Gramma had told her to come. It would be alright, it would . . .

She forced her shaking legs to walk under the swinging sign and through the open door.

CHAPTER 4
The Broken Apple

THE BROKEN APPLE was crowded, its air thick with the smells of stale beer, pipe smoke, and food. Taking a moment to gather both her bearings and her courage, Irvana wove through the tables and benches to the bar at the back of the room. She glanced around, wondering whether her presence would cause a stir, but everyone seemed more interested in the contents of their cups or plates than a nervous girl.

Men were standing two or three deep at the bar as they waited to be served. There was no way to attract the barmaid's attention—Irvana couldn't even see the woman. Instead, she squeezed her way between the men to get closer to the bar.

"Excuse me," Irvana called, but her voice was lost among the deeper ones of the men.

She tried shouting a little louder, but the barmaid ignored her and carried on serving, exchanging empty glasses and coins for tankards full of beer. Irvana didn't have any money, but she did have an idea. When an empty glass was set down on the bar near her elbow, she snatched it up and waved it in the air. It worked like a charm.

The barmaid leaned towards her. "Aye?"

"I am looking for Matteuw, was told he would be here."

"'Ang on." The barmaid lifted her chin and stared out into the room. "Is there a Matteuw 'ere?" Her voice cut like a knife through the din of shouted laughter. "Matteuw?"

A few customers looked round, pausing in their conversations to see who would answer the summons. No one did. They turned their attention back to food and company and the noise level rose again.

"No sign of 'im. Can't help more, unless you want a drink?"

"N-no thank you," Irvana stammered. "It's Matteuw I need. Are you sure he doesn't work here? My grandmother said—"

"I knows no one of that name workin' in the Apple, m'dear, and I've been 'ere for twenty year now. If your man worked here before me, 'e must be as old as the cliff, prob'ly even dead. Al'righ'! I'm comin'! A stout and a Grizzler's is it?" The barmaid hurried away to serve a man banging coins impatiently on the other end of the bar.

Matteuw wasn't here! Irvana stared at the rows of bottles stacked behind the bar, seeing none of them. Why wasn't he here? Panic rose in her chest, closed around her lungs, and she gasped for air. Was Matteuw really that old? Older than Gramma? She'd died . . . was he dead too, like the barmaid said? Irvana gripped the bar tightly as her knees buckled. Her one chance in the city, her opportunity to find out about her parents . . . Gone. What was she going to do now?

She felt a sharp tug on her sleeve.

"You're looking for Matteuw?"

The hand that grabbed her arm had bones that showed quite clearly through paper thin skin covered in age spots. Irvana lifted her eyes from the hand to the face of its owner. The man was wrinkled and wizened like a nut and peered at her through watery eyes. His top lip puckered up towards his nose, showing the yellow teeth which jutted over his thickened bottom lip. A bald dome shone above a few clumps of wispy hair and large ears stuck out either side of his head.

"That's me," he said.

"Really?" Irvana looked for the barmaid to check if the man was telling her the truth, but before she could ask, the man tugged her sleeve again.

"She knows me only as Shaker, on account of this." He held up trembling fingers. "But I was christened Matteuw, and I worked here 'til I broke more glasses than I could clean. Come. Sit with me now you've found me." He beckoned Irvana to follow, but she hesitated.

Was this really Matteuw? He seemed harmless enough as he worked his way past the mismatched stools and chairs set at tables towards a cushioned bench seat on the far side of the room. Perhaps he just wanted company and had decided to pretend to be who Irvana was looking for. As the old man sat down and reached for the mug set on the table in front of him, Irvana decided she'd risk it. At worst, she'd have only wasted some time talking to a lonely old man. At best . . . who knew? So she took a seat on a wobbly stool by the table instead of sitting next to him. Just in case . . .

The man she hoped might be Matteuw took a great slurp from his mug and wiped the dribbles from his chin. "So. Why is a young girl, a stranger, looking for an old man like me?"

Irvana took a deep breath. "Did you know Gwendara, who used to work here?"

He nodded slowly and leaned back in his chair, rearranging his face into what Irvana hoped was a smile. "Aye, I did. She worked here until her husband died, then she left us."

He knew Gramma! Irvana leaned forward eagerly. Could he really be . . . ?

"Brokenhearted she was," he continued. "Freyd was her soul mate. Gwendara was always kind to me, you know, even though I'm not pretty to look at. Unlike many others who were fearsome cruel."

There could be no doubt; Irvana had found Matteuw.

He took another slurp from his cup. "How is she?"

Irvana tried to tell him, but the words got stuck in her throat, forcing her to swallow hard. Then she tried again. "She's dead."

"Ah. 'Tis sorry I am to hear that."

Matteuw stared into the depths of his cup for so long, Irvana thought he'd forgotten she was there.

She touched his arm. "Matteuw, before she died, Gwendara told me to find you. She said you'd be able to help."

Matteuw peered into her face. "Help? Why should I help you when we've only just met?"

Irvana shrugged. "I don't really know. Because you were friends? Because she was my gramma?"

The old man's eyes widened and he choked on his drink, coughing and spluttering. A few heads turned in his direction, but they soon looked away as he recovered.

"How's this? I may be old, but I'm no fool." Matteuw shook his head. "How could she be your gramma? Gwendara had no children."

Irvana stared at him in disbelief. "Of course she did. She had Rolan. I'm his daughter."

"Rolan?" Matteuw looked utterly bewildered. "I'm telling you she never had a son. And Gwendara must have been more than fifty year old when she left here, well past childbearing age."

"But she said you took me to her after Rolan drowned. You arrived one day with me, a baby in a basket—"

Matteuw's agitation increased. His hands trembled so much, he could barely hold the cup. Golden beer slopped down his shirt.

He slammed the cup back onto the table "Me? What a trick for her to play from beyond the grave. I don't know who your grandmother was, girl, but it wasn't Gwendara. She never had no children and I certainly never took no child to her." He frowned. "Per'aps you're a fairy child, come to befuddle me in my last years. Or is this some new form of begging, which takes advantage of an old man? Get away from me . . . go on!" He pushed his chair away from the table so hard, he almost fell as he tried to stand.

Irvana was too shocked to move.

The barmaid hurried over and planted her hands on her hips. "Now then, Shaker, what's all this noise? You knows you 'as to behave yoursel'."

Matteuw pointed an accusing finger at Irvana, making her shrink back in her seat. "It's her, trying to spin me a sob story. And it's all lies!"

The barmaid turned on Irvana with a fierce expression.

"I think you'd better go, especially if you're upsetting my customers. Be off now, and don't come back. Else I'll call the constable."

Irvana didn't need a second bidding. She fled.

CHAPTER 5
The Hiring Stand

OUTSIDE, THE CROWDED square seemed to close in on Irvana. There was nowhere to run to.

She skidded to a halt and spun around on the spot, looking for a way out, looking for answers to the questions that were whirling through her head. How could Gramma not be her grandmother? Had she lived a lie all this time? Was that why Gramma had refused to tell Irvana about her parents, because she didn't know? How then had a baby come to be living with a lonely old woman? Had Irvana been stolen from her real family? And how would she find the answers to any of these questions now?

Feeling sick and giddy, Irvana stopped spinning and doubled over, gasping for breath as the crowds flowed round her. What should she do? She knew no one in the city. Matteuw had sent her packing and she couldn't ask Simean and Matild for more help. They'd already done enough. She had nothing to sell, except . . . But she would never be able to sell anything from the box. She couldn't do that to her gramma's memories. Suddenly she remembered a grubby hand, pleading for food, and forced herself to stand upright. No. She would not beg.

The hiring stand caught her eye.

"I'll get a job!" she almost shouted, startling some passers-by. One of them tutted, and Irvana's cheeks grew warm, but her thoughts ran on. A job, yes. She wasn't afraid of hard work. There had to be something she could do to earn her keep.

She straightened her skirt, screwed up her courage, and stood inside the rope boundary all afternoon, but no one offered her work. Other girls were approached but they were all better dressed, older, and appeared to have experience as kitchen hands, ladies' maids, or seamstresses. A plump cook, still wearing her striped apron covered in floury handprints, did ask whether Irvana was any good with pastry, but dismissed her with a wave of her hand when Irvana said no.

As the day lengthened, only a few desperate hopefuls remained in the stand—Irvana was one of them. Her legs were so tired they refused to hold her up and she sank down onto the hard stone. Her stomach rumbled loudly and tears dripped from the end of her nose onto the bundle she cradled in her lap.

"Are you still here?"

The cook had returned. She was standing a little way from the boundary of the stand, arms crossed over her extensive stomach, brow furrowed with concern. A thin girl with a long nose hovered behind her, watching with wide eyes.

Irvana scrambled quickly to her feet, rubbing the tears from her cheeks. "I can't do anything that anyone wants," she whispered.

"Now, now." The cook pressed a large handkerchief into Irvana's hand.

She gave her nose a good blow and wiped her eyes dry, then offered the soggy handkerchief back to the cook.

"Keep it, keep it," the cook said, waving it away. "Have you worked before, child?"

"Only to look after myself and Gramma." Irvana bit her lip to stop it trembling and twisted the hankie into a knot. "She died."

The cook grunted and frowned. "I didn't need two new faces, but . . ." she muttered. "What's your name?"

"Irvana."

"Irvana what?"

"Um . . ."

Irvana what, indeed. Gramma had never told Irvana her family name—she'd have to make something up. A picture of the little cove she'd left sprang into her head and—

"Shore. Irvana Shore."

The cook smiled. "Well then, Irvana Shore. I've a supper to prepare and the vegetables won't peel themselves. Can you peel veg?"

Irvana found herself nodding.

"Good. We've always plenty of them to do in my kitchen. I'll not leave you here this late in the day. Follow me."

Relief made Irvana's knees go weak. She almost sat back down on the stone as she stammered out her thanks.

"You must be eating more than you send to the table, Cook Merty," a man said. "I swear you get bigger every time I see you."

Behind the cook stood a small group of richly dressed men and women. All of them were laughing at the obvious insult, which had been delivered by a pasty-looking gentleman with a waxed moustache.

Merty narrowed her eyes and pursed her lips into a thin tight line. "Master Cristof."

"I see you are employing extra staff ready for the summer season." Cristof examined the girls and Irvana fidgeted, uncomfortable under his scrutiny. Then he smiled and addressed his companions over his shoulder. "Who knows what unscrupulous folk might have taken advantage of these girls, if it were not for the timely intervention of this saintly cook?"

The ladies hid their smirks behind fluttering fans but the men looked on with open amusement. Merty said nothing.

Cristof puffed out his chest and addressed the world at large. "Tonight, I dine with my good friend, Mistress Andela." He inclined his head towards the woman on his arm.

She was quite the most beautiful creature Irvana had ever seen. Long auburn hair curled over the woman's bare shoulders, vividly red against her pale skin and dark emerald silk dress. The green of the dress was a perfect match for her eyes, which were very definitely fixed on the cook.

"My own kitchen staff roast a good honeyed fowl. You

must ask for the recipe, Cook Merty. No doubt it will increase your repertoire." Cristof laughed at his own wit and gave his moustache a twirl between pudgy fingers.

A glint appeared in Merty's eyes. "Oh, I think his lordship is perfectly happy with my repertoire, sir. I daresay he might invite you to sample some of it. *If* you're lucky."

Cristof drew in a hissing breath and his face contorted. He began to bluster a reply.

"Is Lord Terenz expected back any time soon, Mistress Merty?" the lady on his arm interrupted.

"Not for another week yet, Mistress Andela."

Irvana was sure she saw tears spring into Andela's green eyes just before the lady looked down to hide them behind her lashes.

"Come, my dear. Don't upset yourself," Cristof murmured to Andela, who clutched his arm a little tighter. "You've waited so long for him already. What's another week? He'll be back before you know it and in the meantime, I shall do my utmost to keep the smile on your pretty little face. We are all eager to see his lordship and I have no doubt that he will contact us, immediately upon his return to Koltarn."

"Then, no doubt, I shall be cooking for you . . . *if* he does," Merty said under her breath, her voice dripping acid and with a strong emphasis on "if" again.

Cristof's lip curled but he did not reply. Instead, he guided Mistress Andela away, patting her hand in a comforting gesture. But the beautiful lady did not look very comforted to Irvana. The entertainment apparently over, the rest of Cristof's companions allowed themselves to be sucked into his wake and trailed after the gentleman and his lady.

"Well, that told him," Merty said, to no one in particular. "That poor woman. You'd have thought she would have more sense. Shut your mouths, Alexia and Irvana, unless you want to catch flies."

Irvana hadn't realised she'd been gaping. She snapped her

jaw shut, same as the other girl, and stepped out of the hiring stand. She tried to put out of her head all the questions she was dying to ask and followed the fat cook and the thin girl across the square.

Merty halted beside a fish stall, and Irvana took the opportunity to ask one of her questions.

"Where are we going?" she whispered to Alexia.

Alexia looked Irvana up and down, wrinkling her long nose as though there was an offensive smell under it. "To the palace, of course." She pointed to the cream stone walls high above them. "Don't you know that Mistress Merty runs Lord Terenz's kitchen?"

Irvana's stomach sank into her dusty boots.

"It is a great honour to cook for his lordship. I'm to be the new pastry cook. I spent four years with Lady Willor's staff, you know. I'm very accomplished." Alexia wrinkled her nose again. "Whereas it takes any idiot to wield a knife on a potato. You'd better hope Merty likes you, or you'll be out on your ear before the end of the week."

"Girls! We have work to do. Don't stand there in idle chit-chat."

Merty thrust a bundle of fish, wrapped loosely in brown paper, into Alexia's hands.

With a look of disgust, Alexia held them out to Irvana when Merty's back was turned. "I'm not carrying them," she hissed. "Nasty smelly things. They'll taint my pastry. You do it."

So Irvana, clutching everything she owned in one hand and fish in the other, trailed behind Merty and Alexia to where the roads began to climb steeply. She'd be peeling potatoes for Lord Terenz, overlord of Koltarn!

The thought made her tremble.

The further they walked, the steeper the road got, but Merty's pace never slackened. Irvana's legs shook with the effort of the climb but she pressed on, determined to keep up.

It was getting late. Irvana could see the low sun through the gaps between the houses. And what houses they were! Each one seemed grander than the last, as though the higher it was up the hill, the more chance it had of being admired. Irvana stared at them as she walked past, her aching legs forgotten at the sight of polished windows, paved pathways, and tiled entrances. She couldn't imagine ever living in a house like one of these.

And then there were no more houses to admire, just a wall, a high wall, made from the most beautiful pale cream stones and stretching away as far as Irvana could see on either side of a gateway. Huge wooden doors, studded and hinged with brass, were firmly closed to the outside world.

Merty led the girls towards the gateway.

As they got closer, Irvana saw that not all of the wall was smooth. Above the gateway pictures were carved into the stone. There were birds and flowers and twisting vines—and a star, right above the centre of the gateway. She counted its rays—there were seven.

"Old Tolly is the gatekeeper. Don't mind him," Merty told Irvana and Alexia as she rang the brass bell, which hung from a bracket to the right of the gateway. "He's not pretty to look at, but he won't hurt you."

A small shutter opened in the gate and a pair of eyes appeared in the gap.

"Open up, Tolly. I've got the new girls and if you don't let us in, we can't be cooking supper now, can we?" Merty called to the unseen gatekeeper.

With a bang, the shutter closed. Bolts scraped and then, creaking loudly, the door swung open just enough to allow them in. Irvana squeezed herself through. On the other side was a toothless old man who appeared to be bowing to her. When he did not straighten, she saw the deformity in his back which prevented him from standing upright.

"So his lordship will have tasty pastry now, eh? And twice

as much as before, since it seems you've come back with one too many, Mistress Merty." Tolly craned his neck as though he was trying to get a better look at the girls.

"Only one will do pastry. The other will help with the vegetables." Merty's voice dropped to a loud whisper. "The little one had no hope of being taken on, but I wasn't going to stand by and see her have to go begging, was I?"

The heat of embarrassment crept up from Irvana's toes, all the way to her burning face.

"Ah, but you've a good heart," Tolly wheezed. "I hope she'll be glad of the saving once you've put her to work."

"I'll work her as hard as she can, and no harder." Merty beckoned the girls on. "Best close the gate, Tolly," she called over her shoulder. "We're not expecting guests just yet!"

Tolly pushed the heavy gate shut, muttering under his breath. "They'll all come running once his Lordship's here . . . just you wait and see."

Irvana hung back, watching as he twisted his body and struggled to pull the bolt across. He shot it home with a bang and turned to find her still staring at him.

He waved a fist. "Off with you!"

Irvana flew along the path to catch the others up. She saw they were approaching a grand building made from the same pale stone as the perimeter walls. "Is that the palace? It's beautiful."

Merty chuckled and Alexia rolled her eyes.

"That's just the stables, child," Merty said. "The palace is much further on. Our quickest route would be straight through the gardens the other side of them, but servants must keep out of sight so we take a longer path."

Merty directed Irvana and Alexia to a minor track which forked away from the main path and hurried them along it. The boundary wall towered over them to the left and thick bushes blocked any view to the right. The path seemed endless—would they ever reach the palace?

They came to a further divide in the path, and Merty pointed out an ancient oak, its split trunk twisting upwards into the leafy canopy. "This marks the way to the round garden where the veg are grown. It's the only bit of the gardens we're allowed into. Even so, Lord Terenz likes us to collect what we need in the late evening or early morning, when we're less likely to be seen by him or his guests."

And still the path carried on. Irvana lagged behind, trying to catch more than a glimpse of the exotic flowers and lush grass which was sometimes visible through the trees.

"Irvana! This way!"

Merty and Alexia had disappeared. The shout came from around a bend in the path. Irvana broke into a run.

CHAPTER 6
In the Kitchen

MERTY OPENED ANOTHER door in another cream wall. "Home. In you come."

Inside, the three of them passed quickly through a scullery. Irvana had an impression of gleaming crockery above enormous sinks and then found herself in a large kitchen. How different it was to the open fire in the middle of the floor in the driftwood shack which she'd been used to. Here, pots bubbled on a series of charcoal burners and an empty spit hung motionless in a fireplace big enough for a man to stand in. Servants, dressed in navy and white, were busily chopping or stirring or kneading at the workbenches.

Merty took charge immediately. "Tiffan!" she barked. "Smoked fish pie for supper!"

A youth with orange hair and freckles snatched the parcel of fish from Irvana and threw it onto an empty bench.

"Janil! Meet Alexia, our new pastry cook. She'll be sharing a room with you. Take her things along, sort her out a uniform, and show her where her station is because I'd like a tart of bitter apples tonight and it'll give her a chance to live up to my expectations. Rosann, here!"

The girl who answered Merty's summons was dreadfully untidy. Her apron dragged on the floor, her mousy brown hair was escaping from under a grubby white cap, and her hands were red, rough, and deeply ingrained with mud.

Merty pointed at Irvana. "This is Irvana. She'll share with you and help prepare the vegetables."

Rosann grinned at Irvana and motioned her to follow,

wiping her hands on her apron as she led the way to a long corridor beyond the kitchen.

"I'd offer to 'elp carry your things, but I'm afraid I'd dirty 'em," Rosann told Irvana cheerfully. "It's the veg, see? Sometimes I 'ave to dig them up too, so I've never got clean 'ands. Merty reckons I've always got 'alf a pound of dirt under me nails." She opened a door.

Irvana followed her into a small room where two narrow beds had been crammed. Between them was a minuscule table where a pitcher sat in a chipped bowl, a mirror propped behind it. A curtain hung at the window, a battered chest of drawers occupying the space beneath. The sheets and blanket on one of the beds lay in an untidy heap, as though someone had jumped out of it in a hurry; there were none on the bare mattress of the other.

"That one'll be yours." Rosann pointed at the empty mattress. "I've not 'ad anyone to share with yet, an' I've bin here a year. There's a drawer to put your things in. Why don't you do that, an' I'll find you some sheets an' a uniform. Back in a minute." She grinned and shot out of the door.

Irvana sank onto the bare bed, hardly noticing the lumps in the mattress. A single tear leaked from the corner of her eye and she dashed it away angrily. What did she have to cry about? Gramma would have told her to be grateful—she had a roof over her head and a job. What more could she need?

"To know who my parents really were," she whispered.

She caught sight of her reflection in the mirror and gasped. The rock pools back at the shack had never shown her face so clearly. She leaned closer. Was there anything of her parents in how she looked? Her mouth was wide, her nose turned up a little at the end, and she had a slight dimple in her chin. Her eyes were pale blue or grey it seemed, depending on how the light fell. They gazed out from under bold eyebrows and were framed by long, dark lashes. Her hair was dark, untidy, and there were smudges of dirt on her cheeks.

"You have to be strong, repay kindness with hard work," Irvana told the girl in the mirror. With a sigh, she tucked the worst of the stray ends behind her ears and wiped her face clean before stowing her belongings in the empty drawer.

When Rosann returned, they made the bed together. Then Irvana donned her uniform, feeling self-conscious in the unfamiliar navy skirt and mop cap. She followed Rosann back to the warmth and busyness of the kitchen and stopped at the door, suddenly reluctant to step through it. She didn't know what to do. Everyone else seemed to know exactly what was expected of them. Even Alexia was hard at work, already rolling out pastry on a marble slab.

"Irvana, over 'ere!"

Rosann was beckoning from an archway on the other side of the room and Irvana hurried over to her. Through the arch was a small room with a split door, its top half open onto what looked like the courtyard she'd crossed just a short while ago. The room itself was filled with baskets of assorted vegetables, and squashed right in the middle of them all were two three-legged stools.

"I got Tiffan to find one for you," Rosann said. "You sit 'ere, and I'll get what's left to be done tonight, ready for cookin' tomorrow. Just 'tatoes. Last, cos they're dirtiest . . . 'ere's the water in the buckets, see?"

Rosann set Irvana up with a knife and bucket and they began to work on a small mountain of muddy tubers. By the time they reached the bottom of the first basket, Irvana was sick of the sight of potatoes. She peeled until her hands were so stiff and cold from the water, she could no longer hold the knife safely. Rosann took pity on her and insisted on finishing the rest alone while Irvana massaged some life back into her numb fingers.

"You'll get used to it," Rosann assured her. "I've got some goose grease I use at night. You can 'ave some if you like. It don't smell too good, but it 'elps keep the skin from splitting."

Irvana looked down at her hands. Already, her fingers were stained and several of her nails had broken.

A bell sounded, loud and echoing. Irvana almost fell off her stool.

Rosann jerked a thumb in the direction of the kitchen. "That means supper's ready, and I'm 'ungry enough to eat an 'orse. Come on."

Supper was served in a large, airy room, where a spotless table groaned under the weight of steaming tureens and a golden-crusted pie. Straight-backed wooden chairs were set around the table and Rosann gestured towards two empty seats at the end, furthest away from a chair filled with cushions.

"We all 'as our places according to what we do," Rosann whispered. "We sit at the bottom of the table, cos there's no dirtier jobs than ours in the kitchen. Don't sit down 'til cook does."

Merty's glance ran all the way round the table before she lowered herself with a sigh onto her comfortable cushions. She gave a nod and chairs scraped on the stone floor in the rush to be seated. Eager hands lifted lids from dishes and the air was filled with the mouth-watering odour of fish and vegetables.

Irvana was ravenous and piled her plate high. As she ate, Rosann explained who everybody was and their roles within the kitchen.

"The man next to Merty, 'im with the face that looks like 'e's sucking lemons, that's Graym. 'E's in charge of the wine cellars. Next to 'im is Brin, the storeman. Opposite is Sofy; she bakes the bread of a morning. Janil, sitting next to 'er, is cook's number two. Does the fancy stuff, like rosewater jelly and syrup sponges. Over from 'er is the new lass, pastry cook I think they wanted, not sure what she's called—"

"Alexia," Irvana interrupted. "I don't think she liked me very much."

Rosann continued between mouthfuls. "Then there's Tiffan, 'e's good with fish. Next door you've got Lyle, the spitboy. Best job in the world come winter, but terrible 'ot work in the summer, and sitting by me is Perl, whose 'ands are as red as mine though never as dirty, cos she does the washing up. After that, there's you and me. Each in their place, with their own job, though the others get to muck in where they're needed as often as not. It's not a bad life and there's always the chance to move off the veg to proper cooking."

Perl snorted. "You! Move to proper cooking Rosann? That'll be the day. You'll be grubbing in the dirt for years."

Rosann's chin dropped to hide the colour spreading over her face.

Irvana found Rosann's hand under the table and gave it a squeeze. "Well, we'll be grubbing together, won't we Rosann?" she said, her voice carrying down the length of the table. Heads turned to look at the newcomer and she felt a sudden rush of bravery. "I don't mind what I'm doing, as long as I've a friend to do it with."

Rosann smiled gratefully at Irvana as sniggers rippled down the table.

Perl raised an eyebrow in disbelief. "It's what you can cook that counts here, veg girl, not whether you've got friends."

That night, her first in the palace, Irvana lay wide-eyed in the darkness. Her hands had thankfully been soothed by the goose grease, which Rosann had made her rub into each finger. It was not their soreness which kept her from sleep; it was her mind, working overtime. So much had happened in the last two days. Just two days! It felt like years. The life she'd known and the one she'd hoped for had been ripped away by death and lies.

"Oh, Gramma!"

With a little moan, Irvana pushed her face into the pillow to muffle her sobs. Eventually she fell asleep, her cheeks wet with tears.

CHAPTER 7
Terenz Returns

LIFE SETTLED INTO a routine in the days that followed. Irvana's new world became the bedroom she shared with Rosann, the kitchen, and the little room filled with apparently bottomless baskets of vegetables. During this time, she heard all about how Rosann had been accepted for service in the palace.

"There was so many of us, ten, see? Ma couldn't look after us all so she sent me to work. Vegetables was all we could afford to eat, so at least Merty knew she was gettin' someone who knew 'ow to prepare 'em right."

In her turn, Irvana told a misty-eyed Rosann all about a small driftwood shack, a grandmother who had lived by the sea, and a rather more lonely life. The only thing she didn't share was the fact that she knew nothing about her real family. There was no reason why anyone needed to know that. It would just provide extra ammunition for the other kitchen hands, who seemed to enjoy taunting the two vegetable girls whenever the opportunity presented itself. To keep their spirits up, Irvana kept telling Rosann that one day, they would be in the heart of the kitchen, making fine pastries or cooking the fish or fowl that his lordship enjoyed so much.

The days passed. To Irvana, they were a blur of baskets and peeling and scraping, time passing so quickly that she couldn't believe she'd been at the palace almost a week on the day that Merty bustled into the little vegetable room.

Irvana and Rosann looked up in surprise.

"Drat that oaf, Brin! I should run my own stores," Merty said. "Rosann, I need you to go into the city. I've planned

Black Beetroot Pudding, yet I've no beetroot and no liquorice. Quick, girl, take off your apron. Here's two coppers. Run down to Smayley, the herbalist in Oldside, and ask him for a dozen sticks of liquorice. Be back before lunch or there'll be trouble."

Rosann tore off her apron, dropped it onto her stool, and ran out of the door.

The harassed-looking Merty turned to Irvana. "Is it too much to hope that you have any beetroot at all in these baskets?"

"I haven't seen any—"

Merty groaned. "Then you must fetch some. I can't wait for Rosann."

"But I—"

"Just follow the path round by the trees 'til you come to where the path forks and head towards the round garden. You can't miss it. Beetroot's in the bed furthest from the palace. Pull up a dozen good-sized ones." Merty wrung her hands. "We're not supposed to pick in the daytime, but I need to boil the beets. Just be as quick as you can and stay out of sight. Shoo!"

Irvana grabbed an empty basket and ran after Rosann, not even stopping to remove her apron. She retraced the route she had taken on her arrival and turned off the main track at the twisted oak, which took her along a new path towards a high green wall. As she got closer, she could see that the wall was, in fact, a hedge—planted so thickly she could see nothing through it. The bushes had been trained to form an archway within this living wall. She stepped cautiously through it.

On the other side, a gravel pavement curved away on either side. Directly ahead of her, another path led straight from the archway to the centre of the perfectly circular garden, where a fountain splashed water onto glistening slabs.

"Beautiful," Irvana murmured.

She crunched along the gravel path to the fountain. From that point, other paths radiated outwards—like the spokes of a wheel—each leading towards a narrow gap in the dense hedge which surrounded the garden. The segments between the spokes were further divided by concentric circular paths, low clipped box hedge edging the separate growing plots. Feathery carrot tops waved in a light breeze, beanstalks wrapped themselves tightly around their canes as they stretched up towards the sun, and huge leaves promised a glut of courgettes. There were late strawberries, peeping like rubies from under their leaves, hairy gooseberries—both green and red—growing on goblet-shaped bushes, and pink-white stalks of rhubarb. Irvana breathed deeply. It was good to be out in the fresh air and on her own for the first time in a week. She almost forgot why she was in the garden, but the red-veined leaves in a bed to her left reminded her of Merty's request.

Irvana stepped over the low hedge and knelt in the earth. The ground was soft and the beets came out easily enough, and she pulled twelve of the largest ones she could find. She wiped her hands on her apron, hoisted the basket onto her arm, and took a last long look around the garden. How long would it be before she could come back again? She hurried back to the gap in the hedge and stepped through it.

"Oh!"

Instead of the tree-lined path she had expected to see, there was a velvet lawn dotted with flowerbeds. A wide drive cut through the grass, sweeping up to an imposing building. Irvana glanced at the pillars standing either side of its entrance, the decorative chimneys, and the tall arched windows and realised she had come through at the wrong place. She had a horrible feeling that she was looking at the main door of the palace.

"Oh no! Oh no, no, no!"

Irvana ducked back into the garden before anyone could see her and pressed a hand against her chest, trying to stop her heart from leaping out of her ribs. What was she going to do? She couldn't get back to the kitchens that way. How—?

"Stay calm," she said, and forced herself to count the gaps in the hedge. There were only eight. One of them had to be the right one. All she had to do was walk around the outermost path until she found it. But which one was it?

Through the first gap, she glimpsed a view of the sea; the second revealed more lawn and flowers. The third led out to a magnificent lake, shimmering in the sunlight and bordered by weeping willows. At the fourth entrance she thought she recognised the tree-lined path down which she had come.

She picked up her skirts, darted through the gap, and ran straight into something. The basket and its contents flew one way and she fell to the ground the other.

"What the devil? Get up."

She scrambled to her feet but kept her eyes lowered. Two dusty black boots stepped into view, sunlight glinting on the silver spurs at their heels.

"Look at me."

Did she dare to? A little at a time, maybe. Above the dusty boots, black trousers. A belt with a silver buckle fashioned in the shape of the same seven-pointed star which sat above the main gate. Silver buttons on a black jacket and black gloved hands gripping a silver-topped riding crop. Above the collar of a black shirt, the face of a man.

A man scowling at her, his silvery grey eyes unblinking underneath thick, dark eyebrows.

Irvana felt like a rabbit gazing at a fox.

"I . . . I . . ." Words refused to come. She had no doubt in her head who this was. If only the ground would open up and swallow her whole . . .

"My Lord! Are you hurt?" An elderly gentleman hurried towards the black-and-silver man.

"Does it look like I am?" Lord Terenz snapped. "I do not expect to be interrupted in my garden during the daytime, unless it is by those whom I have invited. And this," he waved his hand at Irvana, "is an unwelcome interruption."

"Unlike ourselves." Two other men approached, one tall, one small. Both wore brightly coloured jackets.

The grey eyes had not left Irvana's face. "Who are you, and what business have you here?"

Something cold and hard hit Irvana under the chin, forcing it uncomfortably high. Terenz held her in that position with his riding crop, and she could only stare at him as he waited for her reply. As he inclined his head, apparently studying her, his long black hair fell forward, over his face. With an impatient jerk, he flicked the hair back, revealing a dark mark high on his cheekbone. To Irvana, it looked like a star.

Terenz frowned. In spite of the morning being warm, he shivered. He pulled the riding crop away from Irvana's chin. "Answer me. What are you doing here, girl?"

"I . . . Merty . . . beetroot . . ." Irvana said in a hoarse whisper.

Terenz looked down at the fallen basket and nudged a beetroot with the toe of his boot.

"Merty's preparing a banquet for your return, Terenz. I'll wager a silver coin that Black Beetroot Pudding is on the menu."

Terenz glanced at the man who'd spoken, the tallest of his companions. "That's no excuse, Robat. She knows my ruling about servants and the gardens." He peeled off his gloves, uncovering long slim fingers. On the littlest finger of his left hand was a silver ring, inlaid with an oval stone that was as black as night and etched with a design Irvana recognised. It was the seven-pointed star again.

"Merty's not expecting you back 'til tomorrow," Robat said. "It's a genuine mistake—"

"I am not intending to punish anyone. Yet."

Robat fell silent with a shrug.

"Surprise!"

Irvana gave a violent start as a boy leapt out of the shrubbery.

Robat drew his sword half out of its scabbard but pushed it back again when the boy started laughing.

Irvana couldn't understand it. Why was the boy laughing so hard? No one else was. The scowl on Terenz's face was enough to frighten anyone, but the boy seemed to think it was hilarious, laughing until he cried.

Terenz rapped him smartly on the top of his blonde head with the silver-topped crop.

The boy stopped laughing and flinched. "Ow! That hurt."

"It was supposed to, Mikal," Terenz said. "What on earth possessed you to do such an infantile thing?"

"Well . . ." Mikal said, rubbing his head.

He looked maybe a year older than Irvana, his clothes a miniature version of those worn by the men but streaked with dirt. His jacket, the exact same blue as his eyes, hung open. He wore a grubby white shirt underneath.

"You know you're always saying I'll never catch a deer 'til I can stalk properly? I thought I'd practise." Mikal crossed his arms and looked up at Terenz, his face a picture of feigned innocence. "I managed to catch you, didn't I?"

"Enough." Terenz turned away from Mikal, but Irvana caught the shadow of a smile on his face. "I do not think that you will catch many deer by shouting at them, Mikal. You also need to practise archery and horsemanship, particularly as your tutors have been quick to inform me of your lack of skills in these areas. It appears that you do not listen to them—"

Mikal pulled a face behind Terenz's back.

Irvana giggled.

"What is so funny?" Terenz's face was thunderous as he bent close to Irvana. "I have been lenient thus far, beet girl, but do not try my patience further. Get back to the kitchen, now. Or I will have you whipped."

Terrified, Irvana dropped to her knees and fumbled for the basket. She began to throw the beets into it as quickly as she could.

"Here, I'll help." Mikal took a step toward Irvana.

"You will not." Terenz's tone was icy. "Your scruffy attire may be more suitable for the role of servant than that of a well-bred young man, but you are my ward and will not demean yourself in such a fashion."

"I just thought—"

"Your impulsiveness is starting to annoy me intensely, Mikal. Perhaps it is time I considered how to curb it more effectively. I do not intend to become a laughing stock as a result of your actions." Terenz turned his back on Mikal and faced the men. "Gentlemen, come. It seems we need to announce our early arrival so there will be no more unpleasant surprises . . ."

How Irvana wished she was invisible!

" . . . and I wish to start planning immediately for the entertainment over the summer season, beginning with my birthday on the fourteenth. Mikal, you will check on the horses. I'm sure that time spent in the stables will fine tune your horsemanship skills no end. Make sure you finish early enough to make yourself presentable for dinner."

Terenz strode into the round garden without a backward glance, followed by the other men. Robat, bringing up the rear, ruffled Mikal's hair affectionately in passing.

"It was a good trick, my lad, though I doubt you'll catch any deer with it." Robat chuckled and disappeared into the round garden.

As she stood up, Irvana risked a sideways glance at Mikal. His fists were clenched and two spots of livid colour showed on his cheeks. His blue eyes, which had been sparkling with laughter a few moments ago, had clouded. He saw her watching him and shrugged, before smoothing his hair as though unfazed by what had happened.

Should she say something? "I'm sorry you got into trouble for offering to help me."

Mikal shrugged again. "I'm used to it. I can't always do what I want to when my guardian's around," he said, a hint of apology in his voice. "It's easier sometimes just to do what he says . . ." He stared at Irvana. "I haven't seen you before."

"I've only been here a week."

"Oh." Mikal dug the toe of his boot into the ground. "So . . . what's your name?"

"Irvana."

"I'm Mikal, though you've probably guessed that already." They stood there in awkward silence.

"Merty's expecting me," Irvana said finally. "She'll get awfully cross if she doesn't get the pudding made."

Mikal's face dropped. "I wouldn't mind if you stayed a bit longer so she couldn't. I don't like Black Beetroot Pudding."

Irvana laughed. She was torn—she'd have liked to stay and cheer him up, but she had to get back. "I must go."

Mikal gave a dramatic sigh. "Never mind. I was hoping if you stayed, I could put off going to the stables. If you want to get back to the kitchens, go through that one." He pointed to one of the arches.

"Thank you . . . sir." Irvana dropped a small curtsey before she headed off. It was probably expected of her. She was only a servant, after all. She reached the gateway, and thankfully, it showed the path she recognised outside. She turned for one last look at the garden and saw that Mikal was still standing where she'd left him. Feeling braver now, she gave him a little wave and was pleased to be rewarded with one in return.

All the way back to the palace, Irvana kept glancing over her shoulder, worried that Terenz might reappear. She walked quicker and quicker until she was almost running and she didn't stop until she was safely back in the little vegetable room. She sank onto her stool to catch her breath and let her heart slow its dreadful hammering.

In the flesh, Terenz had been terrifying. Those eyes . . . Irvana shuddered. She hoped that Brin would never forget the beetroot again. She didn't fancy running into Lord Terenz again any time soon.

But . . .

Her cheeks felt suddenly warm. She didn't think she'd mind so much if she ran into Mikal.

CHAPTER 8
The Guest List

ALTHOUGH THE TABLE in the palace's dining room was large enough to seat thirty, tonight there were only four places set. All at one end.

"Merty has surpassed herself," Terenz said, patting his stomach. He poured more wine and raised his glass. "Here's to Black Beetroot Pudding!"

The two men seated with him were quick to join the toast, but Mikal frowned at his own untouched dessert. For some reason, a picture of the laughing servant girl from the round garden popped into his head.

"I need some air," Terenz said, pushing his chair back. "Shall we?"

The men headed towards a bank of glass doors, ignoring the comfortable chairs arranged around the empty fireplace. None of them spared a glance for the banner hanging over the mantel—a seven-pointed black star on a white background.

Mikal didn't want to listen to boring after-dinner small talk, so he stayed where he was, even though it looked as if the sunset was going to be spectacular.

Terenz was silhouetted against a deepening red sky and even from a distance, Mikal could sense the man's power. Terenz did not suffer fools gladly, a fact that Mikal was all too well aware of. He'd lost count of the number of times he'd ended up on the wrong side of Terenz's temper. It was a mystery to him why Terenz had ever agreed to become his guardian, because looking after him seemed to be such an ordeal. Life wasn't much fun at the moment as Mikal was forced deeper into the mould of a man worthy of the overlord's attention. Would he eventually turn out like Terenz's companions? He hoped not.

Was there anything good in Robat or Gant? Mikal rested his chin on his hand and spared them a thought.

Robat was almost as imposing as Terenz, but in a different way. He was a large man, broad-shouldered and thickset. An experienced soldier with short grizzled hair and a heavily scarred face, he had found favour because of his ability to win battles, both on and off the field. He always looked ill at ease in the finery that court dress code required him to wear, evident tonight from the way he'd impatiently unbuckled his jacket and flung it aside as soon as dinner was over. Robat always treated Mikal like a puppy; a welcome distraction at times, but the novelty soon wore off.

Gant, on the other hand, lacked both Robat's bulk and Terenz's authority. He was slim and short with lightly tanned skin unblemished by any violent skirmishes. There was a hint of cruelty about his mouth whenever he smiled and those piercing blue eyes of his missed nothing. Gant had not won his position at Terenz's side by anything so vulgar as fighting; his talent lay in finding information, something that did not require getting his own hands dirty. Gant reminded Mikal of a rat—sharp features, sharp intellect, and a talent for sniffing out rubbish.

As the last sliver of molten sun disappeared below the horizon, Terenz stepped back into the darkening room.

"Mikal, find Niklos and tell him to bring the guest list for my approval." Terenz threw himself into one of the chairs by the fire, calling for Robat and Gant to join him.

Glad of an excuse to escape, Mikal headed to an office further down the corridor, where the door stood ajar. He didn't bother knocking—he could see Niklos seated at his desk, back to the door, totally absorbed in his work. Mikal grinned. Another chance to practice his stalking skills. With the scratching of the quill to hide the noise of his footsteps, he tiptoed across the room.

"Got you!" Mikal slapped the old man on the shoulder.

Niklos started up so violently, ink splattered everywhere. "You did indeed," he said, dabbing at the fresh ink spots on the sleeve of his robe and on the parchment on his desk. "However, may I remind you that I am not a deer? A good job I have not yet started on the invitations and it is merely the guest list I have blotted." Though his face was stern, his eyes twinkled.

Mikal grinned and then remembered his message. "That's why I've come. Terenz wants to know if you've finished the list. He wants to see it."

"Perfect timing. I have just added the last name."

Back in the dining room, night had blackened the windows. The light of many candles, lit in Mikal's absence, were reflected in their panes. Terenz was laughing at something Gant had said as Niklos approached his chair.

"My Lord." Niklos bowed stiffly.

Terenz extended a hand, not even bothering to look at Niklos. He settled himself more comfortably, draping one leg over the arm of the chair.

Mikal had considered reading the list over his guardian's shoulder, but thought better of it when Terenz's face darkened.

"Niklos, who are these people?" Terenz jabbed a finger into the parchment. "I told you to prepare for a celebration of my fortieth year, and these are who you choose for company? I will hardly enjoy myself with Lady Willor, that fat old bat. And Count Malek?"

"He will bore us all to death with tales of his latest business successes and how much he's worth," Gant muttered. "I can determine that information from the Guild of Tradesmen. Much less objectionable, compared to suffering the presence of the Count."

"This list is full of old maids and faded gentry!" Terenz tore the list in half and flung the pieces aside.

"My Lord, if I may be so bold . . ." Niklos seemed to be

choosing his words with care. He clasped his hands together, almost pleading. "It is traditional that there should be a state banquet, and I thought—"

"You are not paid to think, Niklos. That is my job. And hang tradition. I want a celebration with friends. Gant and Robat are already here, and I daresay Andela and Cristof made it back to the city before we did. Andela will know plenty of other young ladies to provide pleasant company. Tell her to choose a half dozen to bring with her. And send for Josef, Kristin, and Lawrenz. We'll have ourselves a party."

"A party?" Robat's dismay was almost comical. "That's fine for the ladies, but what about the men? I've had enough of dressing up and playing nice in Bernea. Why can't we hunt?"

Terenz dropped his chin onto his hand, looking thoughtful. "Hmm . . . why not? I'm sure even the ladies could be persuaded to enjoy a day in the forest. If everyone arrives on the thirteenth, we'll hunt the next morning. Lunch in the forest before returning to the palace, then music, food, and dancing late into the night. So be it!"

Sounded like fun. There was no way Mikal was going to miss this. "Can I come?"

"You're too young, my lad." Robat laughed. "But I'll let you know if I have any success with your stalking trick on the ladies."

Mikal scowled at the old soldier. It was nothing to do with Robat whether he was allowed to go or not. He took a step closer to Terenz. "Please? I'll behave as gentlemanly as I can."

Terenz shook his head. "Robat is right. You're not old enough for the sort of entertainment I have in mind. You may attend the hunt if you wish."

"But—"

"No buts, Mikal. I have given you my decision. Do not ask again." Terenz turned to the waiting Niklos. "You will dispatch the invitations tomorrow." He waved a hand in dismissal.

Niklos made no sign of leaving, and Terenz raised an eyebrow.

"My Lord, this entertainment is not what is expected—" Niklos began.

Terenz held up a hand.

"It is more fitting for one who bears the StarMark—" Niklos said in a rare display of stubbornness.

Terenz almost overturned the chair as he leapt to his feet. "The StarMark! This accursed sign which remains black upon my cheek?" he thundered, jabbing a finger towards his face. "You would do well to remember, Niklos, that the StarMark confers my lordship and my authority."

"I know that well," Niklos said, quaking where he stood. "You bear the Mark, as all the overlords have done . . . But there are many who would discredit you because it has never been verified. They seize upon any chance to defame you, and breaking with tradition is something they will not take without protest. I beg you to reconsider."

Terenz's hand strayed again to his cheek, where it stroked the star.

"I remain unverified, as you are well aware, thanks to my fool of a brother. The StarMark is a sign from the gods, passed down from father to son, which grants me power. I intend to use that power to the full, even without verification. My father may have accepted your counsel in the past and kept you in service so his sons would accept it too, but I do not wish to avail myself of your advice. Things must change." He stepped closer to Niklos and poked a finger into Niklos's chest, punctuating his next words. "I want to host an informal event, with friends, to celebrate my fortieth birthday. Not a formal state banquet. Do you understand?"

Poor Niklos. He was having about as much success standing up to Terenz as Mikal, when he'd tried it: none.

Niklos's defiance crumbled and he bowed his head, shrinking. "An informal event, with friends," he murmured.

"Exactly," Terenz said.

Mikal watched Niklos shuffle out and then glanced at Terenz. The overlord always got what he wanted.

CHAPTER 9
A Second Meeting

THAT SAME NIGHT, Irvana told Rosann all about her encounter with Terenz when they went to bed.

"I would've died on the spot," Rosann gasped. "What was 'e like up close? I've only ever seen 'im from a distance."

"Tall and dark. He's got a way of looking at you, like this . . ." Lit by candlelight, Irvana narrowed her eyes in imitation. "And he treats people badly. It seemed so unfair, to shout at the old man for being worried and scold the boy when he only offered to help."

"I'm sure Mikal's used to that by now," Rosann said. "Terenz took 'im in, see, when 'e was only four year old. I 'eard Merty tell of how Mikal's mother died of heartbreak soon after 'is father was killed."

So Mikal was an orphan too? At least he'd had some time with his parents. Irvana almost envied him for that. "I hope he doesn't grow up to be as unpleasant as his guardian," she murmured, thinking that she'd rather see Mikal smiling than scowling.

"Don't say that." Rosann looked nervously at the door as though she expected the overlord himself to burst in. "Everyone knows what Terenz is like, but 'e's our overlord, the last of a great family until 'e has sons of 'is own."

"Why is he the overlord?"

"Well, it's cos of the StarMark, o' course."

"The what?"

"The StarMark. Didn't you know?" Rosann rolled her eyes. "That's what's on 'is cheek, the black star. Tis said that in the dawn of time, the gods grew tired of men fightin' to be overlord of Koltarn so they granted the power to rule to just one man. An' that man, with 'is sons after, would be marked with a seven-pointed black star, see? But then the sons grew up an' fought with their father for the position, so the gods 'ad to do somethin' to say who was supposed to be in charge. That's when they made the StarChain. Every time the old lord of Koltarn died, the next in line would put the StarChain on, an' 'is Mark would turn, like magic, from black to gold. An' that's 'ow it all started. There's only ever one man with a gold star, which proves 'e's the man for our city."

Irvana crinkled her brow. "But Terenz's Mark isn't gold."

Rosann chuckled. "Some say it's cos of 'is black heart, but it's really cos the StarChain got lost, see?"

This was getting more confusing by the minute. Irvana sighed. "Tell me what happened."

"Well . . ." Rosann plumped up her pillows to make the telling more comfortable. "Terenz is the youngest of two brothers. Timat was the elder and overlord when their father died. Beautiful Mark he 'ad, on the back of 'is 'and. Imagine that, a golden star, like one 'ad dropped out of the sky . . ." She held up her hand, as though picturing what it would look like with a star glinting there. "Anyway . . . Timat was a good man and 'e married a beautiful princess, Ailsa. They were 'appy and soon expecting their first son, but then there was the plague, see.

"The poor princess caught it. She died, the unborn baby too. Timat went mad with grief, left the castle in Bernea and was never seen alive again. They found his 'orse and what was left of 'im in the forest near here . . ." Rosann shuddered. "Terenz was next in line with the Mark, but they couldn't find the chain to make it all official, like. Terenz reckoned Timat took it with 'im when 'e ran away, so everyone was forced to accept that the Lords of Koltarn wouldn't 'ave StarMarks that turned gold anymore." She gave a huge yawn. "It's no matter to me who 'as a StarMark . . . either way, I gets fed and a warm bed an' if I'm lucky, a friend to work with. His Lordship's Mark can be green for all I care." She snuggled further into her bed and pulled the covers up to her chin. "G'night."

Irvana lay awake, mulling over the story she'd just heard long after blowing out the candle and Rosann's breathing became steady in sleep. How strange that Gramma had never, in any of her stories about Koltarn, mentioned the overlords. What would it have been like, to sit next to her grandmother, probably on the shoreline below the shack, listening to tales of golden stars on the skins of men while the real stars twinkled above them in the blackness of night?

Eventually, Irvana fell into an uneasy sleep, where a tall black-and-silver figure stalked through her dreams.

The following morning, as the breakfast of cold meat, cheese, and thick slices of still-warm bread drew to a close, Merty stood up to address her staff.

"Lord Terenz returned to the palace yesterday, a day ahead of schedule—"

A ripple of interest ran around the table. Rosann's eyebrows shot up in mock surprise and Irvana stifled a giggle.

"—and the rest of the staff will be arriving from today. Our workload will therefore increase." There were a few groans from around the table. "In addition, I have received instruction for a social occasion, planned for Lord Terenz's birthday on the fourteenth."

"A banquet!" Alexia's eyes were bright with excitement. "How many will we be expecting? Fifty? A hundred? Will there be lots of important people? I'm sure Lady Willor will be invited, she's—"

"Lord Terenz is not hosting a large event," Merty interrupted, her lips pursed tightly in disapproval. "It is a small affair I'm told, about a dozen only."

Alexia's face fell.

"One of those parties, eh?" Graym said. "Wondered how long he'd be back before he had one of those."

"We are not in a position to judge what type of

entertainment is held," Merty snapped, "but if, as I suspect, Master Cristof has been invited," she paused as several of her staff sniggered, "I'll not give him the satisfaction of saying there is anything wrong with the food from my kitchen. So. Each and every one of you will do your utmost to make the preparations perfect. Do you understand? Hush now," she called down the table as muttering grew louder. "There's nothing to be done about it. Let's get on."

Before Irvana could leave the dining room, Merty stopped her.

"Irvana, I've an extra job for you. There is an old servant who lives here, Aymee. She used to nurse Lord Terenz and his brother. Their father made sure before he died that she should be allowed to live out her last years here at the summer palace. Nowadays, she's confined to her bed and I usually take her food up myself, but over the next few days I'll be far too busy. So you'll do it instead. 'Tisn't a bad job. Just take her a meal morning and evening and she'll be fine for the rest of the day. Bring that, and follow me." She indicated a tray loaded with a bowl of steaming porridge and a glass of milk.

Carrying it carefully, Irvana followed Merty out of the kitchen and into a dark corridor. After several twists and turns, they emerged through a narrow door onto a much brighter corridor lit from above by a series of skylights in the high ceiling.

"We're in the heart of the palace now," Merty told Irvana, her voice hushed.

There were countless pictures and tapestries hanging on the walls. Irvana did not know which to look at first as she followed Merty's swaying girth down the corridor.

"See the picture of the castle in Bernea?" Merty pointed to a painting in an elaborate frame. "A dark place, that."

Irvana couldn't agree more. Thick forest surrounded the grey towers—and was that a jagged portcullis hanging over the shadowy castle gate?

"Terenz will go there as the weather here turns cold and stormy again. He'll shut himself inside with roaring fires to keep warm. Now, we go down past the StarMarks . . ." Merty ushered Irvana through double doors into a wide gallery.

All down one side, sunlight flooded in through enormous windows. On the opposite wall hung life-sized portraits. Irvana almost reached the far end of the gallery before she frowned and looked back at the row of paintings. They were all men, she realised. And every single one of them had a golden star glittering somewhere on his body. One portrait in particular caught her eye. It showed a young man who looked remarkably like Terenz, but whose hair was the colour of polished chestnuts instead of raven black. This man had been painted posing by a table, indicating with his right hand some point of interest on the map spread there. On the back of that hand gleamed the inevitable golden star.

"Timat," Irvana breathed.

The very last portrait was different to the rest—there was no golden star. Irvana hurried past the frame in which the artist had perfectly captured the arrogant stance and menacing eyes of Lord Terenz.

"Once past the blue vase, you must be quiet." Merty indicated an enormous urn, almost as tall as Irvana, standing in a niche. Then she pushed through a second set of double doors. "This is the bedroom corridor," she whispered. "That's Lord Terenz's room."

The back of Irvana's neck prickled as she tiptoed past the overlord's door. It didn't stop prickling until she'd passed another three or four doors on her way to the end of the corridor.

"Here we are, last but one on the left." Merty knocked gently and pushed the door open. Irvana stepped into the half-light of a room unexpectedly gloomy, its curtains still drawn against the sun.

"Good morning, Aymee. How are you? Put the tray down here, girl. She won't bite."

"Who's there?" The voice was faint and cracked, and came from the bed.

"She does not see well nowadays and always asks," Merty told Irvana in a whisper. Then she raised her voice. "It's Merty, Aymee. I've brought your breakfast and a visitor." She motioned Irvana forward, to the edge of the bed.

The breath caught in Irvana's throat. In the bed lay a woman, bundled up in blankets in spite of the growing heat of the morning. How old was she? Eighty? Ninety? A hundred? Aymee's bony hand, knuckles swollen and skin blotched, plucked at the covers. Her milky white eyes turned blindly towards her visitors and she smiled, revealing gaps where she'd lost teeth.

"Here's a pretty young thing, instead of my old bones for a change," Merty said. "Irvana will be looking after you over the next few days, as I have an important party to arrange."

Aymee stirred in the bed. "For his lordship? Is it Timat's birthday?"

Merty patted Aymee's hand. "Nay, not Timat. Terenz."

"Terenz?" The confusion was visible on the old lady's face. "Of course, Terenz . . . I was forgetting . . . my golden prince is long gone. Gone, with his babe . . ."

"Aye, and his wife too. A sad thing." Merty tutted. "Same every time," she muttered. "She's trapped somewhere in the past in her mind, happened after Ailsa and Timat died. She often forgets that Terenz is overlord. Now, Irvana, do you think you can find your way back to the kitchen?"

Hoping that she would remember the twists and turns of the route, Irvana nodded. Merty said goodbye and left Irvana to her task.

"Time for breakfast, then." Irvana took a seat on the edge of the bed and handed Aymee the bowl. It slipped in the old lady's fingers—Irvana snatched it back before the contents slopped onto the bedcovers. "Aymee, can you hold the bowl?"

No answer. Aymee just opened her mouth, like a baby bird.

Irvana was going to have to feed her. She offered a spoon, loaded with thick porridge, into the old lady's mouth. It took a long time before the bowl was empty.

"I'll come back later," Irvana said, "bring your dinner."

Aymee didn't answer, so Irvana picked up the tray and headed back to the kitchen.

Over the next few days, the number of staff in the palace grew. There were so many new faces, Irvana found it impossible to keep track of who everyone was.

She was kept constantly busy, not only with the extra vegetables that needed preparing, but also with the additional task of delivering Aymee's meals. Feeding the old lady became more than a chore. Irvana poured all the love she would have given Gramma into a different frail body. She tried to tempt a feeble appetite with titbits sneaked from her own plate, drew back the curtains, and opened the window to let light and fresh air into the stuffy room, even added colour and scent with a handful of flowering weeds picked from between the slabs in the courtyard. But nothing seemed to help.

There were rare moments of contact, when Aymee passed comment on the food or sniffed the flowers by her bed, but they were few and far between. And it was pointless trying to hold a conversation. Whenever Aymee spoke, it tended to be a monologue about her golden prince, Timat.

There was one morning when Alexia had squeezed a basketful of oranges for a jelly. Acting on impulse, Irvana pinched a glass of the juice. She'd already taken Aymee her breakfast, but perhaps the smell of oranges, so strong, would force a response from her? It was worth an unscheduled trip if it did. But as she reached Aymee's door, she was surprised to hear a man's voice coming from inside.

" . . . was wondering whether you were still with us, Aymee."

Who was that? She'd heard the voice before . . . one of the recently arrived staff?

Aymee muttered something inaudible and the man replied, his voice so loud, Irvana took a step back.

"I am not Timat! I am Terenz, you stupid old woman."

Terenz! A shadow flitted across the gap at the bottom of the door. He was just on the other side of the door—was he coming out? Irvana's heart raced. She didn't want to meet him—not again! The footsteps behind the door stopped.

"My father and brother both continue to make their presence felt, even from beyond the grave." Terenz's voice was shaking.

Irvana held her breath and listened.

"I have to put up with an ancient scribe and a crazy old woman, thanks to my father's dying wish. And Timat's still your golden prince, isn't he? He always was your favourite. You never cared for me like you did for him. See this? I have the shame of being the first overlord of Koltarn to bear a black star instead of a golden one. And my sons will bear the same shame after me, all because of my dear brother, who stole my birthright when he deserted Bernea with the StarChain in his pocket."

Silence. Perhaps now was a good time to make her escape. Irvana took a few tentative steps away from the door.

"But I am a fool, for taking so much to heart my unchanged Mark."

Terenz's voice was softer now. Irvana paused, straining to catch his words.

"The presence of a golden star, although immensely desirable, has not excluded me from a position on the Council. I ought to be proud of that which sets me apart from those who came before, instead of bemoaning the loss of what I never had. I am Terenz, Black Star of Koltarn. No one. No one," he shouted, "can take that from me."

The door banged open, and Terenz almost ran into Irvana.

"What the—?"

She managed not to spill the juice and recovered from her surprise sufficiently to bob a quick curtsey.

"I assume that beverage is not for me?" Terenz said.

"For Aymee, my Lord." Irvana kept her head down and bobbed another curtsey for good measure.

"Then what are you waiting for? Take it in."

"Yes, my Lord." He hadn't recognised her, thank goodness. But her heartbeat didn't slow down until his footsteps had died away.

CHAPTER 10
Yulia

THE DAY BEFORE Terenz's birthday, Mikal was summoned into the overlord's private apartments, where he found Terenz dressed for riding.

"I intend to go down to the city today, to conduct business that can't wait," Terenz said as he grabbed his customary black jacket from a chair. "You will remain here to welcome my guests, who will be arriving at some point this afternoon. Make sure they are comfortable."

Mikal frowned. "Why me? We've got servants to do that. Can't I come with you instead?"

Terenz thrust his arms into his sleeves and pulled the jacket straight. "No. I have asked Robat to assess your swordsmanship while I am gone as I would value his opinion on what, in the words of your tutor, is shoddy blade work. Your time will be spent more productively here."

"Not fair." Mikal kicked out at a chair and wished it was Terenz's leg.

"You're acting like a spoilt child," Terenz snapped, casting him a scornful glance. "I suggest you act more appropriately. I expect a report on your skills, or lack of them, on my return."

The bitterness Mikal felt at being left behind persisted all morning, even up to the point where a procession of horses arrived at the front door of the palace. Somehow, he managed to fix a smile on his face and welcomed the guests as he'd been directed.

"Is Lord Terenz waiting for us in the salon?" Cristof said, helping Andela to dismount.

Mikal shook his head. "He's out. Won't be back 'til later."

Andela's face betrayed her disappointment.

Cristof chucked her under the chin. "Don't you worry, my dear. I'll keep you entertained until his return."

Andela jerked her head away.

"It is very rude of him not to be here when we arrive," another of the ladies said. "How shall we force Lord Terenz to make amends?"

"We shall endeavour to be the most enjoyable company he's ever experienced, so that he'll regret missing even a moment with us," Cristof announced. "Maybe that will cause him to realise the error of his ways, so he will choose to welcome his guests personally in future."

"Perhaps I shall choose not to be pleasant," the lady shot back. "I will sit with a scowl on my face to match that worn by this young man, and bring gloom to the entire proceedings."

Mikal hadn't realised his smile had slipped. He rearranged his face into a more pleasant expression and tried to ignore the laughter which had greeted the lady's observation and exaggerated grimaces.

"Refreshments are ready inside," he told the party through gritted teeth. "Won't you follow me?"

The group entered the palace, chattering and laughing. It appeared that some of the ladies were visiting for the first time, judging by how they reacted to the tapestries and paintings in the corridors. They reached the salon and Mikal paused on the threshold long enough for them to get the "ooohs" and "aaahs" out of their system.

The salon was, apart from his bedroom, Mikal's favourite room in the palace. It was light and airy and decorated with ornate arrangements of plaster fruit and flowers painted so beautifully, for years he'd thought they were real. In fact, there was still a grape or two missing from a bunch near the fireplace—because he'd been tempted to taste them when he was younger.

And the view . . . the gardens were visible through a wall of floor-to-ceiling glass doors which opened onto them, as well as being reflected in a dozen highly polished mirrors. Anyone standing in the centre of the room would feel as though they were surrounded by greenery.

There were plenty of sofas and velvet-covered chaises to provide seating, and cabinets filled with enough curios to interest even the most difficult of houseguests.

Robat and Gant were already there. Much back slapping and hand kissing followed as they renewed old acquaintances and forged new ones, before everyone helped themselves to food and drink from the buffet table and made themselves comfortable.

Before long, Mikal was bored. He couldn't bear to listen to Cristof spouting on about how many new horses he'd got when he'd much rather be down in the stables himself. He couldn't leave though—what would Terenz say? To pass the time more favourably, he grabbed a spare plate and filled it with biscuits. At least with his mouth full, he would be spared having to join in the conversation.

Mikal wandered over to a chair in the corner, half-hidden behind a large cabinet full of ornamental plates. It was a good spot from which to observe whilst passing unnoticed.

He had to admit, the women were stunning. They were all dressed in fine gowns, with sparkling stones dangling from earlobes or glittering on wrists and around throats. The men were hardly plain by comparison. Their clothes were more subdued, true, but the richness and quality of the fabrics more than made up for their lack of bright colour. The only thing which marred the perfection of the scene was Robat's scarred face, although even that seemed to be lending a hint of roguish glamour to the occasion, judging by the number of ladies fawning over him.

Too late, Mikal noticed Andela making her way towards his hiding place. Was she going to make him talk? No, thank goodness. She walked straight past him and stood by one of the open glass doors, looking wistfully into the garden. Her coppery curls were piled high on her head today, and she was wearing turquoise silk.

"Are you hoping to see anything special out there?" Gant, who'd excused himself from the main group, joined Andela at the window. He spoke in an undertone, just loud enough for Mikal to hear from his concealed corner. "The return of our absent overlord perhaps?"

Andela coloured and turned away from the garden. "I'm sure he will attend us directly, on his return."

Gant smiled and leaned against the door frame, brushing something from his jacket. Mikal recognized the gleam in his eye. It always, always meant trouble . . .

"Shall I tell you a story?" Gant ignored Andela's sigh and shaking head, and leaned closer. "It's a tale about a beautiful young lady, who fell deeply in love with the overlord of Koltarn but found herself shunned by the object of her affections."

Andela gasped and spun away.

"Don't you want to hear why?" Gant murmured. "Oh, but you must . . . I can tell you exactly why Terenz is so cold towards you."

Andela hesitantly returned to his side.

Gant nodded with satisfaction. "Well, where to begin? I think . . . yes . . . I first saw Mikal when he was presented to court at Bernea."

What? Mikal's hand—and the biscuit in it—froze, mid-air. He stopped chewing.

"He was two or three, I suppose, I didn't take much notice," Gant continued. "Children are all noise and filth and trouble at that age, don't you think? I do remember that his father, Sevastyan, was like a dog with two tails, showing off his beloved son and heir. He was a very close friend of Terenz's you know, at least until he got married. Mikal's mother, Yulia, well . . . She was the most beautiful woman I'd seen at court in a long time. Pale skin, blue eyes, hair like liquid gold. That's who Mikal got his looks from, you know." He paused and eyed Andela, who was as motionless and as pale as a statue. "Overlords have always been able to take their pick of the women at court. Timat never did of course, he was quite the gentleman and only wanted Ailsa at his side. But Terenz is a man to take full advantage of his position, as you know from your own experience. He decided he wanted Yulia—"

"She was married!" Andela exclaimed.

Gant waved his hand as if swatting a fly. "What of it? It had never stopped him before. But this time, it was more complicated. This was the wife of a friend. To get Sevastyan out of the way for a while, Terenz sent him to subdue the bandits who were roaming the forest and disrupting the trade routes. Fortunately or unfortunately, depending on your point of view, Sevastyan was killed during a skirmish. Terenz acted the grieving overlord magnificently of course, tried to comfort the young widow pining for her husband. But she rejected all his advances." He watched Andela, clearly enjoying her obvious discomfort. "They say she died of a broken heart but in reality, she threw herself from the battlements of the castle in Bernea."

Sudden tears blurred Mikal's vision.

Andela sighed and clasped her hands together. "I wondered why he became so distant . . . I thought my feelings for him were too obvious, that he saw it as weakness and wanted to punish me for it. But in reality, he loved another?"

Gant looked thoughtful. "You know, Terenz will someday need a wife and heir, but I think he still desires a ghost. Perhaps soon though, you will have a better chance of capturing the heart of our esteemed overlord."

"How can I, if what you have told me is true?"

Gant stepped closer and murmured in Andela's ear. Mikal caught only a few of the words.

"The boy . . . key . . . reminder of Yulia . . . Mikal . . . out of the way . . . your many attractions . . . chance to be appreciated."

Gant stepped back, boldly looking Andela up and down like a butcher inspecting a prime cut of meat. He caught her wrist just before her palm made contact with his cheek.

"How dare you," Andela hissed, trying to twist her arm free.

Gant pulled her closer, his knuckles whitening as his grip tightened. Andela winced. "I dare, because I have his interests at heart. And they are not best served by the boy remaining so close. The question has arisen recently of Mikal's continuing education and I believe Terenz is considering some advice which suggested a position for him. In Bernea. Miles from Koltarn." He released Andela's arm, and she rubbed furiously at the marks left by his fingers.

"Really?" Her eyes were wide with hope.

Gant nodded, smiling. "With the boy out of the way, you will be free to exorcise any remaining ghosts. And for the good of Koltarn, maybe our esteemed overlord will turn back to the living—"

Blinded by a red mist, Mikal dropped his plate and launched himself at Gant. Fists flailing, he landed several blows before he was grabbed from behind, arms pinned to his sides. He began to kick then, not caring who or what came into contact with his boots. There was a grunt of pain when his foot found a target, and the grip on his arms loosened. Mikal tore himself free, swung a fist, and felt a vicious stab of joy as his knuckles connected with Gant's jaw. He grabbed Gant's jacket and drew his arm back for another blow.

"Stop!" Robat yelled.

The red mist cleared.

Mikal saw Robat, frowning at him. Then he looked down, at the mess of broken porcelain and spilled food at his feet. Up again, at Andela staring at him with horror. And then Mikal looked at Gant. He was still holding Gant's jacket, still had his arm drawn back ready for a second strike.

Mikal dropped his hands to his sides as he took in the shocked tableau around him. Oh gods, what had he done?

Gant sneered at Mikal as he wiped a trickle of blood from the corner of his mouth. Then he turned away. Dismissing him. Because he was nothing.

It was all too much. Mikal hurtled through the open door and into the garden. He ran and ran and did not stop until his lungs were bursting. Clutching at the stabbing pain in his side, he collapsed into the undergrowth, somewhere on the very edge of the palace grounds.

It couldn't be true—could it? Everything he thought he'd known, about how he came to become Terenz's ward, was untrue? It was almost beyond belief. Sick to his marrow, Mikal tried to remember life before Terenz.

There were broken moments, vague and insubstantial. Wrestling matches with a man who might have been his father. Songs sung at bedtime. By his mother? The metallic ring of his father's spurs on stone and the gleam of a blade, followed by absence. Could he really remember his mother wailing in despair when a messenger arrived with a bloodied jacket, or was that just his imagination? Either way, he remembered that the singing stopped and then even his mother was gone, replaced by a tall dark man who had looked at the young boy with deep sadness and tears in his eyes.

Terenz.

Had the tears been for Mikal's father . . . or his mother?

Mikal dredged his memory for their faces. Tried so hard to remember a detail, no matter how small. That's all he wanted—the curve of a jaw, the arc of an eyebrow, the shape of an ear. But it was no use. He'd been too young. His parents were little more substantial now than a half-remembered dream. Gone. And Terenz had taken them away from him.

Anger replaced grief. Mikal scrambled to his feet and snatched up a large stick. With sweeping strokes, he thrashed at the nettles and brambles, screaming and yelling with each swinging cut. He beat a path through the plants, ignoring his aching arms, his raw throat and the sweat which blinded him.

Exhausted at last, he threw the stick away and looked around. He found himself near the pavilion.

The pavilion had been built right on the edge of the cliff where there was an almost vertical drop to the rocks and sea below. Mikal climbed the steps and leaned out over the waist-high balustrade. His heart hammered in his chest as he looked down. Was this the kind of view his mother had seen—a dizzying drop to the ground, hundreds of feet below—when she had decided she could not bear to live any longer without her husband? Why hadn't she thought of her son? Had he meant so little to her? Why had she left him alone?

Mikal roared his anger and hurt and hate at the sky, dredging the sound up from his core. His voice finally cracked, his body sagged, and he clutched at the wooden rail in front of him. He had to go back, face Gant and Robat—maybe even Terenz—and answer for his behaviour. Would he have to repeat what he'd heard? Hopefully not, but a lot depended on whether Gant wanted Terenz to know how concerned he was over the state of the overlord's heart.

Whatever happened, nothing could change the fact that Mikal's parents were gone, his future tied to Terenz. A dreadful pain was crushing Mikal's heart and he tried to ignore it, focussing instead on the anger burning inside him as he wandered back to the palace.

The sound of voices—laughter even—broke into Mikal's dark mood and he looked up, startled. He was outside the servant's quarters, probably not a suitable place for the ward of Lord Terenz to be, but right now, he didn't care what Terenz thought. The laughter drew him closer to the building, promising to be a balm for his pain.

The sound was coming from a window. Peering through tattered curtains, Mikal recognised the dark-haired girl who had collided so spectacularly with Terenz in the round garden. What was her name?

"I'll get us clean aprons, shall I, Irvana?"

Irvana—that was it. But he did not recognise the girl who had spoken. Another kitchen hand, maybe?

"We'll be presentable then, if 'is lordship decides to thank us in person for all the veg we've finished peeling so carefully for 'is birthday."

Irvana laughed, her smile making the dimple in her chin more obvious. "I don't think he'll bother. He'll be far too busy having fun." She twisted the end of her thick plait around her fingers. "It's not often we have free time. I think I'll wash my hair before dinner."

"There's water already in the jug," the other girl said. "Shall I fetch you a clean cap as well as the apron?"

The curtains moved slightly in the breeze, blocking Mikal's view. He shifted until he could see, but there was only one girl in the room now—Irvana—her back towards him as she untied the plait and shook out her hair.

"Mikal!"

He wheeled around. Terenz was walking towards him. Had caught him spying. Heat flooded Mikal's face. Anger boiled up inside him again at the sight of the man who'd effectively killed his parents.

Someone started singing.

Mikal flicked a glance towards the window.

"You've found something to amuse you in my absence?" Terenz kept his voice low and inclined his head in the same direction.

"A servant girl . . ." Mikal whispered. How he longed to lash out and tear at Terenz's face.

Terenz stepped up to the open window and peered inside. A slow smile spread across his face. But then the smile froze. He fell back as though he'd been struck and something very much like fear flashed across his face.

"'Ere we go—clean cap an' apron and almos' time for dinner," a girl said, from inside.

Terenz cast a last glance at the window, then grabbed Mikal

by the scruff of the neck and dragged him away, heading for the nearest trees.

When they were far enough away not to be overheard, Terenz let go. "What did you see?" he demanded, pacing up and down in front of Mikal.

"Two girls—"

"Nothing else?"

"Nothing. I'd only just looked in when you called me . . ."

Terenz stopped pacing and glared at Mikal. "I am very disappointed. I left you clear orders to see to the comfort of my guests and instead, I find you amusing yourself in the role of Peeping Tom. Disgusting."

"It wasn't like that. I was only—"

"I don't want to know."

Mikal bit back the rest of his reply. The look on Terenz's face meant that no amount of explanation would suffice. Instead, Mikal gritted his teeth and waited. Punishment was bound to follow and he steeled himself for the inevitable.

Terenz took a deep breath. "You will return with me to the right side of the palace immediately. You will redeem yourself with impeccable behaviour this evening or suffer my immense displeasure. I will never find you spying on the servants again and we shall speak no further on this matter. Come." He set off at a blistering pace.

Was that it? No mucking out the stables? No extra sword practice? Mikal frowned. Terenz didn't usually miss an opportunity like this—it was almost as though he was trying to ignore what had happened. Mikal cast a puzzled glance over his shoulder at the little window.

"Mikal. I said, come!"

Mikal ran to catch up, thanking his lucky stars that he'd got off so lightly and wondering what Terenz had seen through the window to upset him so.

CHAPTER 11
Discoveries

THAT NIGHT, MIKAL barely slept. What he'd heard about his parents played over and over in his head until he couldn't bear it. He rose at dawn, bleary-eyed and woolly-headed with only one thing on his mind; he had to know the truth. From Terenz himself.

Before he lost his nerve, Mikal took a deep breath and hammered on Terenz's door. He pounded twice more before he got an answer.

"Stop! For the love of quiet, come!"

He stepped into the anteroom that Terenz used as an office. The curtains were still shut. Mikal blinked and waited for his eyes to adjust.

A figure stirred behind the desk and there was a grunt of recognition. "Mikal . . . what do you want?"

He heard the chink of glass on glass and the soft glug of liquid being poured, followed by gulping. Was Terenz drinking already? A bit early, wasn't it?

"Well?" Terenz said. "What is so important you could not wait to disturb me? I doubt that you've come to wish me happy birthday."

Of course. It was the fourteenth. Mikal stammered hasty good wishes and screwed up his rapidly disappearing courage. "I want to ask you about my parents."

The words hung in the air between them until Terenz rose out of his chair and flung open the curtains. He stood by the window, shielding his eyes as the bright sun flooded in, shining through the almost empty bottle on the desk. "Well? What of them?"

Mikal could not see Terenz's face, but the overlord's body was tense and still.

Mikal couldn't back out now. "Yesterday, I heard Gant talking to Andela. I don't know if what he said was right, but I want to hear the truth. From you."

Terenz dropped back into his chair and leaned forward, steepled fingers resting on his lips as though he were praying, eyes fixed on Mikal.

Mikal tried not to blink. If he did, the spell would be broken and Terenz would simply dismiss him.

Terenz looked away first. He picked up a jewelled clasp lying next to the bottle, and turned it over and over, watching it flash green and silver. "What did Gant say?"

Mikal decided to stick to the facts. That way, his anger and hurt wouldn't rise up and overwhelm him. He hoped his voice wouldn't tremble too much. "That you sent my father to fight, because you wanted him out of the way so you could approach my mother. When he died you tried to make her love you, but she killed herself instead."

Terenz winced.

A hot burst of satisfaction seared deep in Mikal's gut at the hurt he'd caused.

Terenz laid the jewelled clasp aside, still refusing to meet Mikal's eyes. "It wasn't quite as simple as that. Yes, I sent your father to fight. We were being held to ransom by the brigands and needed to take a hard line. Sevastyan was my friend as well as one of my best soldiers. His experience made him the obvious choice to oversee a campaign against the brigands. It was unfortunate he died in the course of his duty, but it's a risk any soldier takes.

"I knew your mother from court, was with her when we received news of his death. Believe me, I did not enjoy watching her pain." Terenz's voice sounded hollow. "Even with all the resources at my disposal, I couldn't stop her from fading in front of my eyes. Yulia ended her life because she'd lost the man she loved and lived for." He closed his hand into a fist. "I tried not to let the circumstances of her death become common knowledge to protect her. Taking one's own life always causes scandal. The few who knew the truth were sworn to silence. I have no idea how Gant found out . . ." He fell silent.

It still didn't answer the question Mikal really needed to ask. "Why did you make me your ward?"

Terenz shrugged. "Your father was my friend. I felt your welfare should be my responsibility—"

"Because you felt guilty for his death, or because you stand a better chance of controlling me than you did my mother?"

"Neither!" Terenz slammed his hand on the desk. "I did it because you were growing more like Yulia every day." He stiffened.

So that was it.

With an impatient gesture, Terenz flung himself out of the chair and strode around the desk.

Mikal willed himself not to back away. He wasn't ready to forgive, but he was beginning to understand. "Did you really love her?"

Terenz gave a short, mirthless laugh. "Love?" For a moment, his eyes clouded. Then his face hardened and he crossed his arms. "Enough of this emotional garbage. I am sending you to Bernea. You will serve as a page to Lord Lenad and will leave as soon as travel plans have been finalised."

"What?" So Gant had been right. Terenz was trying to get rid of him. "You're sending me away? Why? Because you can't bear to look at me and see someone you actually cared for?"

Terenz's hand shot out, and Mikal braced himself for a blow. Instead, Terenz picked up the jewelled clasp he'd been playing with and slipped it into his pocket.

"Don't be ridiculous. It is high time your education was expanded. A position as Lenad's page will be most informative." Terenz drained what was left of his wine and stared into the empty glass.

Mikal gaped at Terenz. Was he really going to ignore

the real issue? He couldn't help looking like Yulia—couldn't Terenz learn to live with that? "But if you loved my mother, really loved her—"

Terenz stopped him with a look. "The subject of your parents is closed. I forbid you ever to speak of them again. Now, to other matters. I cannot spare the time for a hunt as originally planned. You will convey my apologies to my guests when you join them."

Bile rose in Mikal's throat, bitter and sour tasting. Terenz was dismissing him? "And that's it? I ask you about my parents and you order me around like a servant? I hate you!" He spun on his heel and ran from the room, ignoring Terenz's bellow and the sound of glass smashing against the wall behind him.

Mikal ran straight to his room and dragged his trunk out of the wardrobe. He began to throw clothes into it, and tossed books and boots onto the floor nearby. If Terenz wanted him gone, he'd go.

Slowly, Mikal's anger faded, and he sat on his bed, staring at the mess he'd made. Of course he couldn't leave. Not on his own, not yet. But he would. There would be a time when he would be his own master, could do what he wanted. But until then . . .

"Better do as I've been told," he muttered.

He left the mess he'd made and went to find Terenz's guests instead. They were mounted and ready to depart, waiting only for the birthday boy to join them. They saw Mikal and cheered, making the horses shake their manes and paw at the ground, setting their harnesses jingling.

"Lord Terenz asks you to excuse him, but he's unable to leave the palace," Mikal called as his horse was brought forward.

"Ha! You owe me five sovereigns!" Robat roared with laughter and pointed at Gant. "I told you he'd not manage the hunt after last night."

"I've seen him worse. He doesn't usually forgo a hunt.

There's something amiss," Gant muttered, regarding Mikal through narrowed eyes and running his tongue over a thick lip.

Robat laughed again and made ready to depart.

Andela urged her horse closer to Mikal, worry etched deep on her brow. "Is Lord Terenz indisposed?"

Mikal hauled himself onto the saddle. "No. He's too busy."

"What business can he possibly need to attend to, on his birthday?"

"My return to Bernea, perhaps?" Mikal kicked his horse into a canter, leaving Andela and the rest of the riders to follow.

CHAPTER 12
Thief

"THE PICNIC IS packed and gone, and most of the food is ready for this evening," Merty told the kitchen staff as they took a well-earned break. "It'll be all hands to the pump later to make sure nothing goes wrong."

"Will be interesting to see what mood his lordship's in," Graym said. "He wasn't his usual self yesterday evening. Seemed distracted, in spite of the company. Drank more than normal, then had me deliver another bottle to his chamber when he retired. Let's hope he's in a better frame of mind for the party tonight."

"I'm sure I shall enjoy myself immensely."

As one, a dozen staff—including Irvana—looked towards the door of the dining room.

Terenz stood in the doorway, his face in deep shadow. He stepped into the room, glancing round at the startled faces.

Merty quickly stood and offered him her seat.

"No, thank you," Terenz said.

Merty's cheeks reddened and she wrung her hands. "My Lord, welcome. May I, on behalf of everyone here, wish you a happy birthday? I can assure you that preparations are well in hand for this evening. Your guests will want for nothing—"

"I'm here on an entirely different matter." Terenz looked intently at the servants.

Irvana, at the other end of the table, felt an unexpected sense of foreboding. Had she imagined Terenz's eyes resting on her for a moment longer than on anyone else?

Terenz paced around the table. "There is a thief in my palace."

Irvana's gut clenched. A shiver ran over her skin as the other servants gasped and glanced around at each other.

Terenz continued his pacing. "Imagine my shock, to find that on this day of all days, a brooch belonging to my dear departed mother has disappeared. I have already eliminated the rest of the staff from my enquiries. Which leads me here, to the kitchen staff." He paused. A muscle twitched in his cheek, setting the star on it dancing.

Frightened looks were exchanged around the table.

"B-b-but I am sure of all my staff," Merty stammered. "Th-they would not dare—"

"I mean to find what has been taken and will search for it myself," Terenz shouted. "To your rooms. Now!"

Everyone leapt to their feet and pushed their way out of the dining room.

Irvana and Rosann almost fell through the door into their bedroom.

Rosann clutched Irvana's hands, her face pale. "What'll we do? 'Is Lordship, 'ere, in this room of ours. I can't bear it."

"It'll be fine. We've not taken anything, have we? So Lord Terenz won't find his stolen brooch in here. Sit here, with me, while we wait." Irvana pulled Rosann down onto the mattress and smiled at her. But she had lied. It didn't feel like things would be fine at all . . .

Terenz filled their little room with his black-and-silver presence. Rosann's face grew even paler and she and Irvana jumped to their feet, still holding hands.

Terenz closed his eyes, as though he couldn't bear to look at them. He looked dishevelled, almost as though he'd not taken time to shave or put on a fresh shirt since yesterday. Without warning, he ripped the pillows from the narrow beds and flipped the mattresses over, scattering the blankets.

Irvana bit back a cry as Rosann's nails dug into her hand.

"Whose is this?" Terenz growled, pulling the top drawer from the chest under the window.

"Mine," Rosann squeaked.

Terenz emptied the drawer onto the bed and picked through its scanty contents, his lip curled in disgust. Then he pulled out the second drawer. "And this must be yours."

Irvana managed a nod, then gasped as Terenz tipped all of her belongings onto the floor. Terenz flung the drawer aside and knelt beside the untidy pile, his broad back blocking it from view. After what felt like an age of waiting, he rose slowly to his feet and turned around.

"I think I have found my thief," he said.

Irvana didn't understand. He had? Why was he staring at her like that? And what was that, lying in the palm of his hand? A silver brooch, star-shaped, each of the seven rays decorated with sparkling green gems. The object filled her vision and the room spun. "No . . . I didn't . . ."

Rosann snatched her hand away and stared at Irvana.

"Mistress Merty!" Terenz yelled.

Merty poked her head round the door and Terenz showed her the brooch. Then he indicated Irvana with a jerk of his head. "It seems that you cannot be as sure of your staff as you thought."

"No!" Merty looked from Irvana to Terenz and back again. "My Lord, I . . . I never imagined . . . Irvana, how could you?"

Any moment now, she would wake up. It had to be a dream, a really bad one, Irvana told herself. She hadn't taken anything—she hadn't! But she wasn't dreaming.

Terenz grabbed her arm and his fingers felt all too real on her flesh. "I will deal with the thief. The rest of you may continue with your work," he said, dragging Irvana into the corridor.

It's not me, she wanted to scream. *I didn't do it!* But her tongue seemed bound to the roof of her mouth and the silence was too thick to break.

A sharp tug and she was being pulled along the corridor, conscious of the shocked faces peering at her from doorways. In a daze she stumbled behind Terenz as he took her through the palace and along the portrait gallery. There, painted eyes followed her progress, accusing her of a crime she didn't commit.

Irvana barely registered that Terenz had opened a door and thrust her through it.

Free of his grip at last, she rubbed her bruised arm. Where were they? There was a desk and chair by the window. An office? But through a connecting door she glimpsed a four-poster bed . . .

The door slammed shut. A new knot tied itself in Irvana's stomach with every step she heard Terenz take towards her. He circled her closely, his breath warm against her neck.

"You would steal from me," he said.

"No!" she finally managed to gasp. "I don't know how the brooch got into the drawer, my Lord. I didn't take it, I swear."

"You would take everything, beet girl, if you could."

"No!" What did he mean? Irvana didn't understand. "I took nothing!"

"And I won't let you," Terenz said in a low voice. He grabbed Irvana's plait and yanked, hard.

Pain stabbed through her scalp. Irvana grabbed at his hands, trying to stop her hair tearing from its roots. She whimpered as Terenz brought his face close.

"You would take everything . . . everything from me!"

Flecks of spittle sprayed her face.

"I will not let that happen." Terenz let go.

Irvana fell to the floor. She pressed her hands to the back of her head, trying to ease the ache on her scalp.

Terenz dropped into a crouch beside her. He gently touched the dimple in her chin with a slender finger. "No wonder you left me unsettled, that first time I saw you," he said softly. He touched his own cheek, right on the black star. His eyes were filled with a cold, calculating expression.

Irvana trembled as she stared at him.

She jumped at a knock on the door.

Terenz swiftly rose to his feet and moved a step away. "Come!"

The door opened, and the beautiful red-headed lady from the market place stepped into the room. Her smile of greeting faltered, green eyes widening when they fell on Irvana, then they moved away, seeking Terenz.

"My Lord, I apologise if we are interrupting," the redhead murmured, sinking into a deep curtsey just over the threshold. The boy, Mikal, appeared behind her, carrying a large parcel wrapped in linen and tied with black ribbon.

Irvana daren't move. Terenz was still staring at her, ignoring the visitors. She saw his eyes narrow and he blinked once. Then he turned away, tugged on a bell rope, and lowered himself into the chair behind the desk.

"What do you want, Andela? I'm busy."

Andela's smile brightened. "My Lord, I have a gift. I ordered it as soon as I received your invitation and the tailor worked all last night so that it would be completed in time for your birthday. When we chanced to meet Kenil on his way here, to deliver it, I decided to bring it to you myself. I let the others continue on the hunt and Mikal was courteous enough, or maybe that should be curious enough, to accompany me back." She beckoned Mikal forward, took the package from him, and offered it to Terenz.

Terenz leaned back in his chair and ran a finger across his lips. "A present? Hmm. Open it." He gave a quick jerk of his head.

Andela's fingers trembled as she untied the ribbon and drew from the linen wrappings a silk jacket. It was as black as a raven's wing, hinting at green and purple where the light caught it. She laid the jacket on the desk and tweaked a sleeve to lie flat. "I ordered forty stars to be embroidered around each cuff, one star for every year of your life."

Terenz ran his hand over the material, then touched one of

the silver stars with the tip of his finger. "I now have to wear my age? Kenil will need more time to complete your orders as I get older."

Had he forgotten all about her, Irvana wondered? Slowly, she sat up.

Terenz flashed her a look, then his eyes settled on a point somewhere beyond her, near the door. "Ah, Sofan. I have a job for you. But first . . . Mikal, catch!"

"What?" Mikal fumbled the catch and something silver and green fell beside Irvana: the brooch.

"Pick it up," Terenz snapped. "Put it in the small chest by my bed."

Mikal bent over to pick up the brooch and his blue eyes locked briefly with Irvana's. He frowned, opened his mouth, then closed it again and shook his head. He straightened and headed to the bedroom. As Irvana watched him walk away she became aware of what Terenz was saying.

" . . . she is a thief. The stolen item has been recovered, but I want the constable brought here immediately. I will expect her to hang."

Hang? Oh, gods! Irvana buried her face in her hands. Why was this happening?

"My Lord," Andela gasped.

"She will pay the price for attempting to steal from the overlord of Koltarn." Terenz's voice was as cold as steel.

Irvana heard the swish of Andela's skirts but didn't dare look up.

"Forgive me, my Lord, if I speak out of turn. Why not lock the girl up for now and deal with her tomorrow, after your birthday celebrations? Perhaps a night spent in jail will provide sufficient punishment and scare her enough to encourage her to mend her ways?"

Andela was trying to help. Why, when she didn't know whether Irvana was guilty or innocent? A night in jail was still bad—especially as Irvana knew she was innocent—but she'd accept that if it meant she stayed alive. She finally dared to look up.

Andela was standing beside Terenz's chair, one hand resting on his shoulder. Terenz caught hold of that hand, making Andela gasp. She tried to pull away but he held on tightly. A blush of pleasure coloured her pale cheeks as Terenz placed a featherlight kiss on her palm.

"Mistress Andela," Terenz murmured, "your concern does you credit. I will agree to your request . . ."

He would? Irvana shut her eyes and her body sagged. Surely he'd calm down overnight, decide he'd been hasty. They'd find out who the real thief was tomorrow and she'd be safe . . .

" . . . in part."

Irvana opened her eyes.

There was no warmth in Terenz's smile. In that instant, any hope Irvana had shrivelled and died.

"Sofan, lock the girl in the wine cellar overnight. No one is to have any further contact with her. Tomorrow, the constable arrives to oversee the execution." With a vicious tug, Terenz pulled Andela close, until she was almost nose to nose with him. He stared deep into her eyes. "That way, we will all still enjoy the evening ahead of us. Won't we, Mistress Andela?"

"O-of course, my Lord." Andela's smile looked forced.

Terenz released her with an impatient gesture.

Irvana couldn't think, could hardly even breathe. She was going to die. Sofan approached, and Irvana scrambled to her feet, her only thought to get away. Her foot caught in her skirt and she fell. Straight into his arms. Terrified, she pounded her fists against his chest.

Sofan pinned her arms to her sides. He lifted her easily and carried her towards the door.

Irvana kicked at him. "No! It wasn't me! Please—don't! I'm not a thief!" She sobbed as she was carried across the threshold. "My Lord, please!"

Terenz sat at his desk with a strange expression on his face, watching. Then the door closed, sealing Irvana's fate.

She knew that look.

Triumph.

CHAPTER 13
The Truth

IRVANA STOPPED FIGHTING Sofan long before they reached the wine cellar, but he still carried her all the way. No words were spoken, not even when Sofan pushed Irvana through the door and locked her in. She clung to the grille in the door because she didn't trust her legs to hold her up.

Sofan hung the keys on a hook, well out of her reach. "Sleep, if you can."

"I didn't take anything. I'm innocent," she whispered.

Sofan shrugged. "Lord Terenz thinks you're guilty." He took the lamp with him when he left and the darkness grew deeper with every step he took. His footsteps echoed briefly, then all was silence.

Irvana forced herself to let go of the grille. She turned and leaned against the door. As her eyes adjusted to the dim light, she was able to make out the shelves and bottles with which she shared her prison. It was cold—the perfect temperature for wine maybe, but the chill seeped into her bones and the musty smell turned her stomach. She wrapped her arms tightly around her body to stay warm, but only her tears held heat as they slid, unchecked, down her cheeks. She sank to the floor, buried her face in her skirt, and sobbed. What a nightmare. There was no hope for her—Terenz would never back down. Tomorrow, she would die.

Much later, after she had cried her eyes dry and hiccupped into silence, she heard something. The scraping of metal on metal, followed by a definite click. A key was turning in the lock. Irvana scrambled away from the door as it creaked open, her heart racing.

A shadow crept in.

Irvana pressed her back against the closest wall as the shadow drew nearer. A tiny flame flared in the darkness, blinding her.

"There you are!"

She shaded her eyes, trying to make out who was behind the flame. The tiny light went out.

"I'm getting you out of here. Come on."

A warm hand grabbed her much colder one and tugged her to her feet. She was pulled out of the cellar and stood trembling as the door was locked behind her. Another match flared, and this time Irvana saw her rescuer clearly.

"Hurry!" Mikal said.

Irvana fell over her feet as she tripped up a spiral staircase and followed Mikal into the residential part of the palace. She had so many questions, she didn't know what to ask first.

"What are you doing?" she whispered as they hurried through the portrait gallery.

"Shh!" Mikal placed a finger on his lips.

Irvana glanced up at the nearest painting. Terenz stared back at her. "Oh!" she gasped. "You're taking me back. The constable's arrived early."

Mikal seized her arm as she turned to run and pulled her around to face him. "Of course I'm not," he hissed. "I *will* explain, but there's only one place I can think of where it might be safe to do that. Trust me, please."

Could she? Trust him? Irvana wasn't sure, but she allowed herself to be led onwards, every sense alert and prickling, every fibre in her body straining to detect danger. Just as she feared she would burst with tension, Mikal ushered her into another unfamiliar room. He closed the door behind them and let out a sigh of relief.

A four poster bed, hung with drapes of forest green, almost filled the room. What little space remained was not at all tidy. A large open trunk stood in the middle of the carpet.

It was half packed and a mess of possessions were scattered around it.

"I'm going away soon," Mikal said, nodding at the trunk. "This is my room. You should be safe here for a while. Terenz never comes in here if he can help it."

Irvana stared at him, confused. "Why are you doing this? Why did you let me out?" She knew she sounded ungrateful and suspicious, but she needed to know what was going on.

"Because I don't believe you stole that brooch."

"Wh-what?" Irvana blinked, surprised. "I mean, I didn't, but why do you think—?"

"You can't have taken it because I saw him with it, first thing this morning."

Proof that she was innocent! Her bones felt like they were melting with relief—she could escape the hangman's noose. But wait. Mikal saw Terenz with the brooch? But that meant . . .

"He lied? Then why did he say it had been stolen? And why blame me? What have I done to deserve that?" Irvana couldn't keep the alarm out of her voice.

"Apart from crashing into him that time?" Mikal shrugged. "I don't know. But I do know he's lying and I'm not going to let him hand you over to the constable for something you didn't do."

Irvana bit her lip. "If you help me, won't he be angry with you?"

"Not if he doesn't find out. I'm going to leave you here for a while so I can fetch your things. Then I'll find a way to get you past Tolly at the gate so you can hide in the city." Mikal frowned. "Probably best if you get out of Koltarn as quickly as you can, though. Terenz is bound to come looking for you."

Irvana was going to have to leave? The room started spinning. She grabbed a bedpost to steady herself. "Thank you for doing this . . ."

Mikal looked uncomfortable. "Don't thank me 'til you're

safely away. There's still a lot that can go wrong. I'll come back as soon as I can. Stay hidden."

Mikal rushed out of the door and Irvana sank down on the window seat. Hidden behind thick curtains, she gazed out over the garden without seeing it. How had this happened? She'd thought there was a future here at the palace, a chance of a better life. It had all been snatched away. For some reason, Terenz had set her up and wanted her dead. Cold sweat broke out on her skin at the thought. Why? Why would he do that to her? With a moan, Irvana pressed her forehead against the cool glass and closed her eyes.

There was only one person who believed she had not stolen the brooch. She would have to place all her trust in him if she was to stand any chance of getting out of here alive.

But at this moment, all she could do was to wait anxiously for Mikal's return.

MIKAL HEARD SNATCHES of conversation as he crept past the servants' dining room, but he reached the bedrooms unchallenged. Working his way along the corridor, he opened every door until he recognised the furniture in Irvana's bedroom and entered on silent feet.

Someone screamed.

He leapt across the room and pressed a hand over the open mouth. "Quiet!"

Enormous eyes stared at him over the top of his hand. Had anyone heard? Mikal waited until he was certain that no one was coming to investigate.

"Don't make a sound. Understand?" he whispered to the girl.

She nodded.

Mikal took his hand away, ready to slap it back if she made so much as a squeak. He put a finger to his lips and closed the bedroom door. "Who are you? Why aren't you with the others?"

"Oh sir, I'm Rosann. I didn' feel 'ungry after what 'appened . . ." The poor girl looked close to tears. "I can't believe what Irvana's done, won't believe it."

Mikal decided quickly. He hoped he wouldn't regret what he was about to do. "Rosann, is it? Listen, Irvana didn't steal that brooch."

"She didn't?"

Mikal ran his fingers through his hair. How was he going to explain? "No. For some reason, Terenz wants everyone to think that she did. Irvana's got to get away, or he'll kill her. You might be able to help."

"Kill 'er?" Rosann's eyes widened. Then she squared her shoulders and looked fierce. "Tell me what to do."

"Can you pack up her things?"

"O' course! Most of 'em are still on the floor where Terenz tipped 'em out. I'll wrap 'em in this." Rosann grabbed the corner of Irvana's cloak and pulled it from the pile. As it whipped free, a box went flying across the room and crashed against the wall. "Oh! What was tha'?"

"Shh. It's just a box. Pick it up, quickly." Mikal opened the door a crack and peered out into the corridor.

Rosann moaned, and he glanced over his shoulder at her. She was kneeling on the floor beside the box, its lid open and some of its contents scattered around it.

"Irvana must 'ave taken the brooch. Look, she took Lord Terenz's ring as well."

"What? Let me see." Mikal felt sick. In two strides he was beside Rosann and snatched the glittering object from her fingers. Had he been mistaken? The girl was, in fact, a thief? Fearing the worst, he looked the ring over. It was gold, set with a deep blue stone engraved with the familiar seven-pointed star. "It's a StarRing, all right . . . but not Terenz's. His is silver and black."

"But . . . but StarRings are only given to boys with StarMarks." Rosann looked puzzled. "No one'd dare to 'ave a ring wi' the star on it unless they was supposed to."

Mikal's mind worked at lightning speed. How could there be another ring, when Terenz was the last of his line? "Give me the box. I don't know who this belongs to, but I know someone who might. Pack everything else and take it to my room. You know where that is? Irvana's there. Do it as quick as you can and wait there until I come back."

He dropped the ring into the box and darted out, leaving Rosann kneeling, bewildered, on the floor. He sprinted through the palace, his only aim to reach the man he thought might be able to identify the jewellery. He burst through the office door without knocking.

Niklos dropped his quill. "Mikal, whatever is wrong?"

"Irvana . . ." Mikal bent over, out of breath.

"Who?"

"The servant girl. From the round garden. Terenz accused her of stealing a brooch, ordered her to hang."

Niklos tutted his disapproval. "Stealing is a serious crime, Mikal. There must be consequences to prevent others from following in her footsteps."

"But she didn't steal it." Gods, why couldn't the old man understand? "She couldn't have taken it because I saw Terenz with it, just this morning, watched him put it in his pocket. He must've planted it in her room. I don't know why. But she's not a thief, I'm sure of it."

"Why on earth would he do such a thing?" Niklos said, getting to his feet.

"I don't know, but this might have something to do with it." Mikal took the ring out of the box and offered it to Niklos. "It was in Irvana's belongings."

Niklos staggered two steps back and clutched at his chest. "A servant girl had that ring?"

"Yes. It fell out of this box."

Niklos recovered and stepped forward swiftly. "What else? Is there anything else in there?"

Mikal flipped the lid open. "Just bits and pieces. What were you hoping there'd be?"

"I don't know . . ." Niklos took the ring from Mikal and turned it this way and that. "The last time I saw this ring, it was on the finger of . . ." He shook his head. Were those tears shining in the old man's eyes? "Where is the girl now?"

"In my chamber. I let her out of the wine cellar—"

"Then take me to her," Niklos ordered. "Immediately."

THE BEDROOM DOOR creaked open and Irvana's heart began racing again. Was it Mikal, at last? Please, don't let it be Terenz . . . She peeped around the curtain.

"Mikal! You took so long, I was worried—" She pulled back the curtain and her stomach dropped like a stone.

Mikal wasn't alone.

"It's fine, don't worry," he said, hurrying to her. "This is Niklos. He's got something to ask you."

"I didn't do it, I swear," Irvana said. How many more times would she have to say it?

"Please, calm yourself." The old man she'd last seen in the round garden smiled. "I merely need to clarify certain aspects of this situation. May I join you?" He gestured towards the window seat.

Was he here to help? Or was he looking to prove Terenz's case? After a moment's hesitation, Irvana shifted along the seat, making room for one more. Niklos eased his creaking limbs onto the cushion with a little groan. Then he beckoned Mikal forward, took something from him.

"Gramma's box!"

Niklos placed it in Irvana's lap, and she traced the flowers on the lid, surprised at the dull ache in her heart. She hadn't felt that for a while, had kept both the box and her emotions hidden.

She frowned. "Why have you got this?"

Niklos cleared his throat. "Do you know what the box contains?"

Irvana nodded. "I think they were Gramma's reminders of happy times."

"Hmm." Niklos looked thoughtful. "Do you recognise this?" He held out the gold ring with the blue stone.

Again, she nodded. "It was in here." She tapped the box gently. "I think it might have been my grandfather's."

"I don't think so."

Niklos shook his head, and Irvana's stomach gave a lurch. Not Freyd's? Was she about to be accused of another theft?

"This ring belonged to an overlord," Niklos told her. "It's a StarRing."

The words echoed in Irvana's head as she stared at the ring. The scratches in the blue stone rearranged themselves into an ordered shape—a seven-pointed star.

"You said this was your grandmother's box. Was she your only family?" Niklos asked.

Irvana blinked at him, trying to concentrate. "Yes. Well, I thought she was. Until . . ."

"Until?"

"Until I came to Koltarn."

"Please, explain."

Irvana felt her cheeks flush with shame. "The man Gramma said would help me told me she'd never had a son, so I couldn't have been her granddaughter," she whispered.

"I see."

There was judgement in the silence that followed. Tears prickled Irvana's eyes—her secret was secret no longer.

"Well," Niklos said eventually, "whatever her relation to you, I wish she'd told you how she came by this ring. If only she had brought it back to Koltarn . . . I'm sure Lord Terenz would have rewarded her generously. It belonged to Lord Timat, you see, Terenz's brother. He would have been wearing it when he died . . ."

"Timat?" She knew that name. "The golden prince?"

Niklos looked sharply at her. "What's that?"

"It's Aymee. She calls Timat her golden prince."

"Of course." Niklos jumped to his feet, a feverish light shining in his eyes. "I wonder if she can remember the night he left Bernea? Quickly, come with me." Still holding the ring, he hurried from the room.

Mikal grabbed Irvana's hand and pulled her after Niklos. Aymee's room was only at the end of the same corridor, but to Irvana it felt as though it took forever to reach it.

Inside, the old lady was hunched under her blankets, apparently asleep.

"Do we wake her?" Irvana whispered.

"We can't ask her anything if we don't," Mikal said.

Irvana stepped closer to the bed. "Aymee? Aymee, it's Irvana. I've brought someone to see you."

It took a while, but eventually Aymee responded.

"Do you remember me?" Niklos stepped closer too. "I am clerk to the overlord."

Aymee's milky eyes turned towards his voice. "Niklos, the young clerk? I remember you."

"Not so young now." Niklos chuckled. "Aymee, do you know what this is?" He took her hand and placed the ring into it.

Aymee felt it over carefully, tracing the star with a fingernail. All of a sudden, her face lit up. "His StarRing! It's come back." She held the ring close to her eyes, as though trying to see it better. Then she pressed it to her lips.

"May I?" Niklos prised the ring from her bony fingers. "Timat was wearing this when he left, wasn't he? After Ailsa died?"

Aymee nodded. "Took his treasure . . . he wept bitterly over it . . . I thought his heart would break. I saw the ring—"

Niklos nodded. "Just as we always suspected. Timat's treasure—he took the StarChain."

"—when he took the babe from me."

"The what?" Niklos looked as though he'd been slapped.

"Tiny . . . brought to birth early . . ."

A baby? What baby? Irvana tried to remember. There hadn't been a baby in Rosann's version of the story . . . it had died with the princess. Yet now, Aymee was crooning a lullaby and rocking an invisible child in her arms.

"Ailsa had the baby after all?" Niklos looked relieved. "So Timat didn't desert us willingly. He must have been trying to outrun the plague which killed his wife, aiming to reach Koltarn and isolate himself and his son. That's why he left."

Something niggled at Irvana. "Rosann said Timat died in the forest. That's where Gramma lived."

"Ooh! I bet I know what happened." Mikal wagged a finger at Irvana. "Your grandmother found Timat when he was dead or dying and took the ring. That's how it got into her box."

Niklos and Irvana looked at each other. She saw his eyes widen and he turned back to Aymee, a new note of urgency in his voice.

"Aymee! Did the baby have a StarMark?"

Aymee hugged the imaginary baby closer to her chest. "There, there, sweeting, one day it'll be gold like Papa's . . . when you're a lady and wear your hair up, they'll see it then. Now hush, hush while Papa gets on his horse . . ." Her words became an incoherent mumble and she slid back under the bedclothes.

"The baby arrived early and soon after, Ailsa died," Niklos muttered. "Timat, mad with grief, fled to protect his greatest treasure. His heir."

"But if Timat died, the baby couldn't have survived—" Mikal began.

"It must have done," Niklos snapped. "Don't you see? Irvana's grandmother must have found Timat, presumably dead or very close to dying at that point. She took his ring and something even more valuable." He rounded on Irvana. "How old are you?"

Why was he looking at her like that, his eyes boring into her? "T-twelve. Thirteen, come winter," she stammered.

"It fits—it all fits. The woman you thought was your gramma discovered Timat's priceless treasure. Not the StarChain. A baby." Niklos took a deep breath. "She found you."

Irvana heard the words, but none of them made any sense.

Mikal grabbed Niklos's arm. "That's not possible. The StarMark is carried by sons, not daughters."

Niklos shook his arm free. "It has been carried by girls, though it is an exceptionally rare event. There have been no recorded cases for the last three centuries. We can confirm the theory only by the presence of a StarMark. And I think Aymee has just told us where to find it." He looked at Irvana.

All the pieces suddenly fell into place. Irvana went cold as she realised exactly what Niklos was suggesting. "Me? You think Timat was my father? But I don't have a StarMark! I would know if I had."

"Not if it's where Aymee said."

She shook her head. "This is stupid. You've taken a few facts and some wishful thinking and turned me into someone I'm not."

"Please, let me look."

She didn't want him to. She didn't want to know—or did she? Because if she knew, then the mystery of her parents would be solved too. Irvana clenched her fists tight and nodded. Niklos took the weight of her plait in his hands and lifted it up. *Let him be wrong. Please, let him be wrong*, she prayed.

"There is a star, right here."

In spite of the warmth of his fingers, Irvana shivered as Niklos touched the nape of her neck.

"It's much smaller than Terenz's and hidden by your hair. No one would see it unless you cropped your hair short."

The expression of undisguised joy on Niklos's face made Irvana feel light-headed. She had a StarMark? Her own face probably mirrored the shock on Mikal's—his mouth hung open and his eyes were round as marbles.

"That's why Terenz wants you out of the way," he blurted. "He's seen it."

"Never. How can he have seen it? It is too well hidden," Niklos said.

Mikal shook his head. "He's seen it, I tell you. Yesterday, when Irvana was washing her hair."

Mikal had been watching? What else had he seen? Irvana's cheeks grew warm as she remembered slipping out of her uniform.

"It's not as bad as it sounds," Mikal muttered, staring at the floor, his own face reddening. "I heard you say you were going to wash your hair and saw you undo your plait. But Terenz found me, outside your room. He looked through the window and acted really strangely afterwards. If he saw your StarMark, he wouldn't waste any time in trying to get rid of you."

"That's no way to speak of your guardian," Niklos interrupted. "We have no proof—"

"No proof? Today, he's accused Irvana of stealing that brooch—"

"—and ordered me to die." A chill rippled down Irvana's back. Mikal was right. Terenz knew. He had discovered the truth about Irvana before she had managed to find it out for herself.

It seemed he did not intend anyone else to know.

"If this is all true, if you are Timat's daughter, then *you* should be overlord of Koltarn, not Terenz," Niklos said. "This makes it imperative that we act immediately. He has managed thus far to hold onto power because Timat had no heir and Terenz's opponents are not strong enough to depose him. But if he really does know about you . . ." He didn't need to say anything else.

From what she'd overheard outside Aymee's room only a few days ago, Irvana knew that Terenz would not hesitate to remove any threat to his position as overlord.

Danger pressed in from every side, making it difficult to

breathe. Irvana expected a black figure to leap into the room and seize her. Mikal must have felt the same, judging from the nervous glances he cast about.

They left Aymee and hurried to Niklos's office. Behind closed doors, Niklos sat at his desk and dropped his head into his hands. Mikal stood beside him, chewing at a thumbnail. Irvana? Well, she might have looked calm, but inside . . .

There might be noble blood coursing through her veins. She could certainly feel every drop of it, pumping through her frantically beating heart. The daughter of an overlord? Impossible. Why hadn't Gramma told her anything about her birth? Had she not understood what the ring meant when she took it from Timat? Or had she understood perfectly well and chosen to hide it? Had Gramma ever thought of trying to take her back, or just kept her in the hope that if such a tiny scrap survived it would help to ease her own heartache?

They would never know, and it didn't really matter now.

Irvana's hand strayed to the back of her neck but she couldn't feel the Mark, even though she now knew it was there.

Niklos sighed, breaking the tense silence. "You must go to Bernea, attend the Council. But first we must inform the Prime Minister of our discoveries and ask for protection on the route. It will take several days for a letter to reach him and for his reply to return. We will need to disappear while we wait for an answer."

"We?"

Niklos straightened his shoulders. "I shall accompany you and present your case to the Council. It is my duty, as clerk to the StarMarks of Koltarn. I can hide you in the city, at least for a while. In a small property I purchased recently."

"But if you leave today, at the same time as Irvana, won't that look suspicious?" Mikal said.

"You're right." Niklos nodded thoughtfully. "I shall have to invent an excuse, join Irvana later."

Mikal snapped his fingers. "Here's an idea. Terenz is sending me back to Bernea soon. What if I asked for you to accompany me? He won't let me travel unaccompanied. Instead of going straight there, we pick up Irvana on the way."

"It might work, but I don't know . . ." Niklos looked doubtful. "If Terenz found out . . ."

"He won't, I promise. He'll probably be glad to see the back of me."

Niklos eyed him. "Why? What have you done?"

"Me? *I've* done nothing." Mikal fiddled with the buttons on his jacket.

"Really?"

Mikal blew out a breath. He explained what he'd discovered about his parents and why Terenz wanted him gone.

How strange that they should both have discovered the truth about their parents at the same time. For Irvana, the truth had opened up the possibility of an unimaginable future but for Mikal, the knowledge had caused nothing but pain.

"So that's why I don't want to be anywhere near him either," Mikal concluded.

Niklos's eyes flicked between Irvana and Mikal as he frowned in thought.

What would he decide? Irvana chewed her lip. She didn't quite know why, but she wanted Mikal to come to Bernea with them too.

"Very well." Niklos's manner became brisk and businesslike. "Mikal, you've given us the excuse we need and it's probably our best chance of escaping detection. Irvana, you must collect your possessions—"

"Already in hand," Mikal said. "I asked the girl you share a room with to pack your things. She'll bring them to my room as soon as she's able."

"Good." Niklos turned his attention to Irvana. "How well do you know the city?"

"I don't." Her stomach churned. How was she ever going to find the safe house?

"Right. Mikal, go to the library. Find a map and copy it so that Irvana can find this address." Niklos scribbled hastily on a piece of parchment. "In the meantime, I will write the letter for the Prime Minister. Irvana, you must hide."

CHAPTER 14
A Broken Mark

CARRIED ALONG ON a wave of other people's decisions and powerless to do anything to help, Irvana found herself back in Mikal's bedroom again, hiding behind the curtain. So many people taking risks because of her. Niklos. Mikal. Even Rosann. She hadn't meant for any of this to happen. If only Terenz had never seen her Mark . . .

Waiting now was harder. The silence was deafening, filled with worries about things she couldn't control. The heavy curtains were stifling her, she had to open them, get out . . . In an effort to distract herself, Irvana paced the room. She picked through an assortment of odd-shaped stones, a couple of broken arrows, and some loose feathers on top of a chest of drawers. She lifted a book from the untidy stack on a shelf and thumbed through the pages, but there were no pictures and she could not read it. She knew only enough letters to recognise and write her own name. After dropping the book back onto the stack, she skirted round the open trunk and its related mess. Lying on Mikal's bed, where she'd left it, was Gramma's box.

She reached out to pick it up and the door behind her opened. She spun round.

Terenz! Standing in the doorway!

Fear crawled from her toes, up her legs, and settled in her stomach like a lead weight.

Terenz's grey eyes were like magnets, holding her captive.

"How did you . . . ?" Angry colour flooded Terenz's face as he pushed the door to behind him. Then he covered the distance between them in a few easy strides and raised his hand.

Pain exploded in Irvana's head. White lights flashed in front of her eyes and her cheek burned, red hot. Did she hit the floor? Perhaps. She wasn't there long—a vice-like grip closed on her throat and lifted her up. She tried to prise it free.

"I think it is time for you to disappear for good, beet girl."

The stranglehold tightened. Irvana clawed desperately at the hand crushing her windpipe. She couldn't breathe, there was no air. The white flashes in her vision multiplied until she saw only a glittering tunnel with Terenz's smile at the end of it. The smile disappeared, swallowed up by darkness. She was falling, falling through deepest blackness towards a tiny spot of pure white light.

A shudder of impact ran through Terenz's hand.

Irvana was released. She fell back, gulping at the air, trying to shake the darkness from her head. As the blurred edges sharpened and colour came back to the world, she thought she must be dreaming.

Terenz lay on the floor beside her. Motionless. Bright red blood stained the carpet beneath his head.

"I've killed 'im!"

Irvana blinked, trying to focus on the speaker. Was it really Rosann, her face ashen, Gramma's box gripped tightly in her hands? Rosann dropped to her knees by a bundle of clothing that looked vaguely familiar. From somewhere, Irvana found the strength to drag herself away from Terenz and throw her arms around Rosann, clinging to her like a drowning sailor clings to driftwood.

"What the devil—?"

Irvana looked up and couldn't force the words past her swollen throat as Niklos and Mikal hurried into the room. Niklos crouched beside Terenz, his knees cracking loudly in protest as he reached to take the overlord's pulse.

"I killed 'im!" Rosann's voice rose with hysteria. "I grabbed the box and I 'it 'im . . ."

"He is not dead." Niklos's tone was sharp. "But you have knocked him senseless."

"The blood—"

"There is a gash on his cheek, that's all."

It was true. A deep gash ran straight through the centre of Terenz's black star.

Irvana was paralysed by the sight of blood, dripping steadily onto the floor. Hands lifted her, helped her to sit on the bed while Niklos tried to stop the bleeding. How her throat ached. And her tongue seemed to be stuck to the roof of her mouth . . .

Rosann's voice sounded as though it was coming from a long way away. "I snuck up 'ere to bring the clothes, like you asked. When I got 'ere, 'is 'ands were round 'er throat. I 'ad to stop 'im. 'Er lips were blue, so I grabbed the first thing I saw and 'it 'im. 'E dropped like a stone."

Gods, he'd so nearly killed her. Irvana buried her face in her hands.

"This changes everything," Niklos said, his voice shaking. "Rosann, I'm sorry. There is no time to pack. You must leave with Irvana. Immediately. Before Terenz recovers."

CHAPTER 15
The Safe House

IRVANA SCRAMBLED OUT of the bedroom window behind Rosann, terrified that at any moment she would feel the grasp of long fingers, adorned with a silver ring, on her back. She caught a brief glimpse of Mikal's pale face as he pulled the window shut. Then he disappeared.

He hadn't said a word—not a single word—to her, since he'd seen Terenz lying on the floor.

"Irvana. C'mon," Rosann whispered, urgently.

Irvana ran into the lengthening shadows after Rosann. They darted across lawns and veered around flower beds, aiming for cover.

Deep in the trees, Irvana had to stop. "Did anyone see?" she gasped, clutching her aching sides.

Rosann peered out over the garden. "Can't 'ave done. No one's after us at any rate. We mus' keep goin', mus' get to the gate."

They ran along the hidden servant's path until they reached the gate through which Irvana had arrived such a short time ago. They hid nearby, crouching behind a rusty tin bath propped against the wall of the gatehouse. Rosann looked for the old keeper while Irvana caught her breath and massaged her still tender throat.

"I don' know if the gate's locked," Rosann whispered. "But if it is, I knows where Tolly keeps the key."

The clanging of the gate bell almost deafened Irvana. She pressed herself as close to the wall as she could. Would the bath be big enough to keep them from being seen? Shuffling footsteps announced Tolly's approach. After a cursory glance through the little shuttered window, he laboured at the bolts.

The gate opened and Robat rode through, the body of a fine stag slung across his saddle. The rest of the party followed *en masse*, their horses' hooves stirring up the dusty ground. Tolly coughed and almost disappeared from sight as the dust rose above his head.

"'Old your breath."

"What?"

Rosann pulled Irvana into the choking dust cloud.

The stone archway loomed over Irvana's head and then they were through it and running. She heard a dull thud behind them and they skidded to a halt and looked back. Tolly had closed the gate.

"We did it," Irvana gasped.

Rosann grinned shakily. "A fine sight we mus' look, covered 'ead to toe in dust. I 'ope it don' make us stand out."

Irvana looked down. Her skin felt gritty and there was dirt on her clothes. She tried to brush the worst of it off. "We don't look too bad, but it would be best if we didn't hang around. Can you remember where we've got to go?"

"Course." Rosann recited the address Niklos had made her repeat half a dozen times. "Let's go."

Arm in arm they hurried down the steep road. The narrowing streets were filled with deep shadows and strangers. Every patch of darkness seemed to hide a potential threat, every adult who passed might be ready to question them. And every time they turned a corner, Irvana expected to see the black, silver, and bloodstained figure of Terenz waiting for her.

They found Niklos's house as the sun set. It was tall and thin, tucked away in the depths of the city and squashed into a row full of similar houses. The front door opened directly off a busy street with a small marketplace at one end and a maze of dark alleys at the other.

"Hurry up," Irvana hissed as Rosann fumbled in her pocket for the key. They were completely exposed.

"Got it." Rosann held up the key and pushed it into the lock. Then she turned a panic-stricken face to Irvana. "It won't turn."

Irvana's knees buckled. Were they at the wrong place? A cold sweat broke out between her shoulder blades.

But then Rosann gave the key a jiggle, it turned and she pushed the door open.

Irvana tumbled thankfully inside.

THE NEXT FEW days were a living nightmare. Irvana jumped at every new sound, she barely ate a thing and slept only fitfully. She was exhausted.

Rosann dared to go out to buy food and firewood, but Irvana didn't set a foot outside either of the doors. Fear of recognition and capture kept her trapped inside as effectively as the key in the lock of the wine cellar had. Things had felt better when she had a full stomach and had warmed up, but her nerves were stretched to breaking point as she waited for a knock on the door that meant they had been discovered.

Irvana became familiar with every room of the house. The kitchen was on the ground floor. It had two doors; the one they'd unlocked, which opened onto the narrow street, and one on the opposite side of the room, which opened not onto a garden or yard as she might have expected, but another strip of alleyway.

Stairs led from the kitchen to a large room on the first floor with a bay window overlooking the street side of the house. From here, the stairs wound up to two bedrooms on the second floor and an attic room under the roof.

On their third day in hiding, it rained steadily. Irvana's spirits were as damp as the cobbles outside. She was alone again, as Rosann had had to go out to replenish their dwindling stocks of food. Curled up in a chair, Irvana stared at the flames dancing in the fireplace. How much longer would it be, before Niklos came and they could leave?

The rain came down heavier, the drops pattering against the window. Irvana glanced at the water running down the glass. Then something harder than rain rattled against the window and she sat up. Were they stones? Who would throw—?

She jumped up to see. Two familiar figures stood dripping in the street below, a couple of trunks and a bag at their feet. They were here! At last!

Irvana thundered down the stairs into the kitchen. Half-laughing, half-crying, with fingers that trembled in their haste, she unbolted the door and pulled it open.

"About time. I didn't think you were ever going to hear us." Mikal hauled the trunks over the threshold and stepped inside. He shook himself like a dog, showering Irvana with droplets of rain.

She took Niklos's bag and helped him out of his damp coat. "I'm so pleased you're here. I thought you'd forgotten us."

"Forget you? Never. This was just our first opportunity to get away." Niklos peered at her. "Are you unwell?"

"No, just tired." Did she really look that bad? "Rosann will be back soon and we can get something to eat. Come on upstairs, it's warmer."

Niklos settled himself into the chair that Irvana had vacated and Mikal stood close to the fire, his damp trousers steaming.

Irvana chose the floor at Niklos's feet, where she sat with her hands clasped together to stop them trembling. "Tell me, what's happened since we left?"

"Well, Terenz came to, not long after you escaped," Niklos began.

"He was furious," Mikal said. "Kept yelling for people to find the thief. When they couldn't find you or Rosann, Niklos suggested that maybe you'd been working together. He said Rosann must have been the one who got you out of the wine cellar and you'd attacked Terenz when he disturbed you both in the act of ransacking my room—"

"Ransacking your room?" Irvana gave a snort of laughter. "Most of the mess you'd already made."

"Well, at least it served a purpose. No one would've taken Niklos seriously otherwise."

"First time I've ever heard such a good excuse for a mess."

"Now then. No arguments," Niklos said. "Terenz accepted my theory. He couldn't have done otherwise without admitting the truth—that he'd discovered Timat's heir and tried to murder her. The birthday celebrations continued as planned, only slightly marred by his injury."

Mikal burst out laughing. "You should have seen Andela. I thought she was going to faint when Terenz appeared, his face a mass of bruises. She insisted on staying on to look after him and has been all over him like a rash ever since. At least that meant his attention was on something other than us leaving. I don't think he even noticed I'd gone."

Was there a hint of bitterness in his words? Irvana thought the answer might be yes. "Surely it's better that way?"

"It's not that simple, I'm afraid," Niklos said with a wry smile. "Terenz is still determined to find the so-called thieves. He's not stopped looking, you know."

"He's still after us?" Irvana jumped to her feet, heart leaping in her chest. "Rosann! What if—?"

"Calm yourself, child. She's a sensible girl, won't take any risks. She'll be back soon, safe and sound."

But she couldn't be calm, knowing that Rosann was somewhere in the city, in the rain, with Terenz still looking for them. She paced the room, wringing her hands.

Niklos sighed. "Do you know how to play Tacala, Irvana?"

She stopped mid stride and gaped at him. "Ta-what?"

"It's a game. Might help to pass the time, keep your mind occupied. Mikal, will you teach her? I think there's a board in the cupboard there . . ."

How could learning to play a game possibly help? For a start, Irvana couldn't concentrate and the basics of the game were definitely not as easy to master as Mikal would have her believe. Her frustration built. Then Mikal captured yet another of her counters.

"I give up," Irvana said. "I'll never understand how to play."

"You'll soon get the hang of it. You're not doing so badly. Let me set them up again—"

"No!" Irvana swept the counters off the board. They rolled in all directions. She pushed her chair away from the table and went to the window.

"I'll pick them up and put them away then, shall I?"

She ignored Mikal and looked out into the street. The rain had eased and it was getting late. Even at this time of day, there were still plenty of people out and about—how she envied them their freedom. One of them was running along the narrow street, weaving in and out of the crowd. Irvana leaned closer to the glass, peering through the raindrops which distorted her view.

Even as she recognised Rosann—running as though her life depended on it—the kitchen door crashed open below, slammed shut again and Rosann came pounding up the stairs.

"Soldiers! Coming down the street. They're coming here," Rosann panted.

For a moment, no one moved. Irvana glanced out of the window, saw the glint of light on metal helmets. One of the soldiers pointed out the house and his companion looked up—straight at her.

She shrank back, her hand pressed against her chest to keep her heart from hammering its way out of her ribs. "Terenz! He's found us."

"Upstairs. Now," Niklos ordered. "They mustn't suspect your presence if their enquiries are innocent. Mikal, hurry, get that board put away. Rosann, back downstairs, see if you can delay them."

Irvana flew up the stairs on near silent feet and burst into the bedroom. Somewhere to hide, there had to be somewhere she could hide . . . under the bed? In the wardrobe? Someone pounded on the street door, then she heard heavy steps running up the stairs.

"Please, please make the soldiers go away," she whispered.

There was the sound of muffled voices below. A shout of surprise.

What were the soldiers doing to her friends? They mustn't hurt them—not when it was all her fault they were here. Irvana hauled the door open and almost fell down the stairs in her desperation to reach Mikal and Niklos. She froze on the bottom step and stared.

One of the soldiers had taken hold of Mikal's shoulder and his free hand was reaching out for Niklos.

Irvana launched herself at the soldier. She tugged at his coat, trying to pull him away. "Don't hurt them, please."

The soldier gave her a surprised, but not hostile look. Uncertain, confused, Irvana let go of him and looked at her friends. Everyone was smiling. Smiling?

Niklos took her hand. "It is not what it seems."

She could only stare at him.

"All is well," Niklos said. "Please, allow me to introduce the son of a very old friend of mine. This is Captain Davith. Davith, this is the girl we believe to be Timat's daughter, Irvana."

Something like a cloud passed over Davith's hazel eyes, darkening them, but it was gone so quickly, Irvana decided she had imagined it.

Davith gave her a smart salute. "It is a great honour to meet you. May I assure you of my loyalty to the StarMarks of Koltarn?" He placed his right fist over his heart and bowed.

"Then you weren't arresting Niklos or Mikal . . ."

Davith shook his head. "Not at all. I am here on behalf of the Prime Minister."

He was a friend, known and trusted by Niklos. Irvana

dropped into a chair and passed a trembling hand over her face. All was not yet lost.

"But now to business, I'm afraid. I have something to deliver." Davith slid a hand inside his jacket and withdrew a thick letter.

Niklos broke open the seal on the parchment and began reading.

Davith took his helmet off while he waited and rubbed a hand over his close-cropped silver hair.

Irvana studied him. So he wasn't as young as she'd thought he was, in spite of his high cheekbones and square jaw. There were streaks of dirt and dust on his cheeks, dark shadows under his eyes and at least a day's worth of stubble on his chin—signs of the journey he'd taken to reach them, perhaps?

"You will be escorting us to Bernea, then." Niklos folded the letter up.

"Indeed." Davith smiled briefly. "I am ordered to make all possible haste while attracting as little attention as possible, if such a thing is doable. To that end, as I am the only one aware of the true nature and importance of this assignment, I left my lieutenant outside the house and the rest of my men are waiting beyond the city walls."

"Good, good. We appreciate your discretion." Niklos pursed his lips. "Will it extend to the rest of our little party? There are four of us travelling you see. One is Mikal, who I'm certain you've already recognised."

Davith nodded. "I take it that Lord Terenz is unaware of your involvement in Irvana's case?" he said to Mikal. "Even though you have a legitimate reason for heading to Bernea?"

"Yes. And it needs to stay that way." Mikal's tone was firm.

"It will." Davith's tone was equally firm.

"Good." Niklos beckoned to Rosann, who must have crept up the stairs from the kitchen. She bobbed an awkward little curtsey.

"And this is Rosann. She'd been out to fetch something for our supper I believe. Will you join us in a meal?"

"I would have enjoyed that, but I am afraid we must leave tonight. Supper will have to be a cold one, eaten in the coach. I am certain it will be excellent, nonetheless." Davith shot a smile at Rosann, who blushed. "I can allow you very little time to make ready. Travelling in a closed carriage, overnight, I am confident that we will arrive in Bernea by tomorrow evening.

"Is it wise to travel at night?" Mikal sounded uncertain. "There are bandits in the forest—"

"There will be ample protection," Davith said. "I would trust my men with my life, and they will fight to the death under my command even if they do not know who it is they are protecting. I will order the carriage to be brought as close as it can be to this address and return to escort you to it, as the Prime Minister wishes me to keep a close eye on Irvana. Remember—you have very little time and must be ready when I return." He performed a perfect salute, dazzled Irvana with a smile, and turned crisply on his heel, replacing his helmet as he ran down the stairs.

It was silly, but Irvana missed him already. Somehow, in the short time he'd been with them, she'd felt so much safer.

"You need to be aware that the Prime Minister is somewhat doubtful of your claim, Irvana." Niklos tapped the letter against his leg, a frown darkening his face. "He asks that you be kept from public view and that the Mark should remain hidden until he can examine it himself."

"Huh! Eran wouldn't recognise the truth if it bit him on the—"

"Mikal. That's enough. Eran is being cautious, and rightly so."

Mikal swallowed the rest of his comment and even had the grace to look a little ashamed of himself.

"We must get ready to leave. At least we didn't unpack . . ." Niklos stuffed the letter into his pocket. "We will need the StarRing close to hand. Irvana, can you wear it?"

She thought back to the first time she'd opened Gramma's

box and tried it on and shook her head. "It's far too big. I'd lose it before we even left Koltarn."

"Then it must be hidden, but within easy reach."

"What if it were sewed into Irvana's clothes?"

Everyone looked at Rosann.

Rosann shrugged. "Most folks carry their valuables in a strongbox or wear 'em. We 'aven't got a metal box and it can't be worn where folks would think o' lookin', so we sew it into a seam. No one'd think o' lookin' there, would they?"

Niklos clapped his hands together. "Ideal. Irvana, there's a sewing box in the corner . . . Mikal, you can help Rosann pack food for the journey."

She was going to Bernea. Going to Bernea. The words kept time with the needle as Irvana sewed, all fingers and thumbs in her nervousness. Eventually she snapped the thread and inspected her handiwork. Someone would have to look really closely to notice the fresh stitches in the deep hem of her skirt.

There was nothing any of them could do now, except wait for Davith.

CHAPTER 16
The Road to Bernea

THEY WERE READY when Davith returned a short time later.

Irvana pulled the hood of her cloak up as she stepped outside, hoping it would be enough to hide her face from any curious citizens who were still out and about. She hurried along the narrow street in the gathering darkness. With Davith striding beside her, the small trunk containing her possessions clamped under his arm, she knew she would be safe, but there was still a strange tightening in her stomach and an iciness in her spine. She quickened her steps, eager to reach the carriage, and slipped on the still damp cobbles.

Davith caught her as she pitched forward. "Steady. Are you alright?"

"Yes, thank you . . ."

Davith's hands were warm, his grip strong. "Careful then. I don't want you to break your ankle."

They finally reached the deserted market place, and the coach was waiting. It bore no distinguishing marks and was quite unremarkable in its ordinariness. Davith opened its door and wedged Irvana's trunk under the seat before waving them inside. Niklos boarded, Rosann too, but Irvana held back.

She was on a path she could not change, had no control over what happened next. But she had to do it, had to find out what the future held for her if she really was Timat's daughter. She took a deep breath and clambered on board. "Where's Mikal?"

"He has decided to sit up top, with his trunk." Even in the growing darkness, Davith's teeth shone white as he grinned. "I believe he thought it would be too good an adventure to miss."

"Until 'e gets too cold and miserable, I'll bet," Rosann said. "Then 'e'll want to be back in 'ere, with us."

Davith grew solemn. "The journey will not be comfortable. The road is rough and we shall be travelling as fast as we are able. The full moon will help, although it will do little to speed our progress through the deepest parts of the forest. I shall follow to the rear until the rest of my company joins us outside the city. I suggest you try to sleep." He slammed the door shut.

The inside of the coach was plunged into deeper darkness. Outside, harnesses jangled and there was the murmur of voices—Davith speaking to the driver.

"Forward!"

With a jolt, they began to move, the coach rattling through the near empty streets.

Irvana sank back into her seat. It seemed such a short time since she had arrived in Koltarn on the back of Simeon's cart, and now she was leaving. Secretly, in a closed carriage. With an armed escort. In between her arrival and departure, she had found a job and lost it, discovered a new family to replace the one she'd always thought was hers, and almost lost her life. She shivered. Whatever lay ahead in Bernea, good or bad, whether she was the daughter of an overlord or not, she would face this new challenge the same way she'd faced everything else.

The ride became quieter but noticeably bumpier and Irvana knew they must have passed beyond the city walls. The coach came to a brief halt, and Rosann risked a peep out of the cloth-covered window.

"There's a load more soldiers outside," she reported.

Irvana peered over Rosann's shoulder. The smoke from a dozen torches streamed upwards into the night sky, illuminating extra guards.

They travelled deep into the night. As tiredness overtook them, Niklos fell to sleep, his gentle snores interspersed

with the thud of hooves and creaking of harnesses, and
Rosann curled up like a cat in the corner. Only Irvana found
it difficult to rest.

What if the evidence was wrong and she wasn't who
Niklos thought she was? He'd presented a convincing case,
but if her Mark was not a true StarMark . . . What punishment
would Terenz devise for someone who dared to challenge his
position? All manner of consequences, each more dire than
the last, played through her mind until exhaustion got the
better of her and she settled into an uneasy sleep.

A shouted warning jerked her awake. The coach juddered
to a halt and silver moonlight washed over her as the door
flew open.

"Well, what 'ave we here?"

Silhouetted in the opening was a giant of a man. Something
glinted in his hand—a knife. Ice dribbled down Irvana's spine.
Bandits! The intruder lunged forward and seized her wrist
with a rough hand.

Irvana screamed.

Niklos shouted and grabbed her attacker, trying to break
his hold on her. The bandit didn't even look at the puny arms
wrapped around his waist. He simply rammed an elbow into
Niklos's belly. Niklos grunted in pain and sat down, hard, on
the bench seat.

The grip on Irvana's wrist slackened. She pulled free, caught
her foot on the trunk, and fell. Her head struck something
hard and the world turned black before filling with sparkles.
She pushed herself up and aimed for the open door, pain
dulling her senses. Must get away . . . Danger . . . She reached
for the doorframe and grabbed a handful of curtain.

"Not so fast. C'mere."

Strong arms caught Irvana around her waist. The curtain
was wrenched from its fittings as she was flung back into the
coach.

Niklos leapt at the bandit again. Suddenly, his face sagged
and he collapsed.

Irvana screamed again at the sight of the bandit's knife, its blade dark and wet.

The man reached out to grab her again. Then he grunted and the knife fell from his hand. In slow motion he folded up and slumped heavily onto the floor of the coach.

"Got him!" Mikal threw down a tree branch and grabbed the man's legs. "Help me, quickly."

Gritting her teeth against the throbbing in her head, Irvana pushed while Mikal pulled. Together, they managed to haul the enormous body to the door and shove it out. The bandit hit the ground with a dull thud, audible even above the sounds of fighting.

The world outside was all confusion. Torches were where they had fallen, lighting up the feet and legs of fighting men. Screams of pain cut through the shouts and clash of metal on metal. Horses reared in fear, their riders slashing wildly at the men seeking to unseat them. It was impossible to tell friend from foe.

"The driver's fighting. Hold tight, I'll get us away!" Mikal leapt out and slammed the door shut behind him.

Irvana heard a scrabbling on the roof, the crack of a whip, and the coach gave a great leap forward.

Niklos groaned.

"He's bleedin'," Rosann shouted.

In the now curtainless carriage, moonlight lit the dark stain spreading across Niklos's stomach.

Irvana shook her head, trying to clear it of the sparkles at the edges of her vision, and fought to reach Niklos over the motion of the carriage. She held him close, cushioning his body against the jolts. She had to stop the bleeding, but how? She pressed her hand against where she thought the wound was and warm wetness seeped between her fingers—blood. Bile rose up in her throat and she swallowed it down.

The sound of fighting grew fainter. They'd got away—they were safe. For one glorious moment, Irvana almost believed it. But then—oh gods! A horse, following them. Getting closer . . .

"They're coming after us," Rosann gasped.

Irvana pushed Niklos away and snatched the bandit's knife up from the floor. They wouldn't take her, not without a fight.

The coach slid to a halt for a second time. Irvana tightened her grip on the knife, holding it at arm's length. If only her hand would stop shaking . . .

The door slammed open.

Davith's eyes burned almost as fiercely as the torch in his hand.

Irvana let the knife fall. Wordlessly she reached out to him. Flickering light lit her bloodied hands and skirt.

"You're hurt? More torches. Quickly," Davith roared.

"Not me . . . Niklos," she managed, as Davith thrust his torch at another soldier and leapt inside.

"'E's been stabbed," Rosann added.

"What?" Davith pushed Irvana aside and bent over Niklos, deftly examining his wound. "This was not supposed to happen."

"Are we pursued?" Niklos asked weakly.

"No. The bandits have been dealt with. Not many survived to run back into the forest." Davith's face was as grim as his words. "Medic, to me."

"Was it a planned attack?" Niklos persisted. "Are we discovered?"

Davith didn't answer. Someone handed him a leather bag—he opened it and thrust his hand inside. Irvana caught a glimpse of white fabric and glass bottles. Davith pulled out wads of cotton wool and tightly rolled bandages and worked swiftly, padding and strapping Niklos's wound.

Irvana watched his face as he worked. Davith was an experienced soldier—he must have seen men wounded before. Why then was his face so pale in the torchlight? Perhaps, she reasoned, as she did her best to wipe Niklos's blood from her hands, perhaps it was different when it was a friend who lay injured. And she knew Davith was a friend of Niklos . . .

"They knew we were coming," Mikal said.

Irvana looked up, startled. Mikal was peering in, his face green-tinted at the sight of so much blood.

"Don't be ridiculous," Davith snapped. "Bandits will always attack when the opportunity presents itself. And that's all they were—outlaws." He dropped his voice. "Apart from myself and Eran, no one else knows about Irvana yet. No one."

Niklos tried to speak, but his voice was weak. Davith and Irvana leaned closer, trying to catch his whispered words.

"Terenz does." Niklos closed his eyes with a groan.

Davith frowned. He checked the bandages one last time and rested his hand on Niklos's shoulder for a moment or two. "Don't exert yourself, my friend. Lie easy." He turned to Irvana. "Keep him as warm and comfortable as you are able. I won't stop again unless we have to. We need to get to Bernea, quickly." He glanced at Niklos's bandages, where a fresh stain was already showing. "Mount up!" He pushed his men aside as he jumped down from the carriage.

"Are you sure you're all right?" Mikal asked.

Irvana nodded and he shut the door, enveloping her in velvety darkness, relieved only by a patch of light where the moon shone through the uncovered window.

It was a lie. Irvana was nowhere near all right. How could she be? She'd been attacked by a knife-wielding bandit, witnessed Niklos being stabbed . . . and it all pointed in one direction. Towards Terenz. Had he known all along of their plans? Been observing them all this time, waiting until exactly the right moment to attack and make her disappear for good?

"Irvana . . ." Rosann's voice shook.

Irvana groped for Rosann's hand, and felt her friend's fingers tighten around her own. On the seat opposite, Niklos moaned quietly.

"What can we do for 'im?"

"I don't know."

Niklos's injury was serious, Irvana had seen it in Davith's

expression. She had no idea how long it would take before they reached Bernea and proper help. All she could do was pray for the bleeding to stop.

The coach moved, leaving the battle behind, but the feeling of horror stayed with Irvana, a tangible presence in the darkness.

Niklos stirred. "The locket . . . you must . . ." His fingers fumbled at his jacket buttons, struggling to undo them. When the jacket fell open, it uncovered a silver necklace. He winced as he passed the chain over his head and held the locket out to Irvana.

"Keep it safe. She used to wear it . . . right over her heart . . . was never without it." He fell back, his face grey and beaded with sweat. "Don't think badly of me for keeping it . . . With this close . . . I could bear my loss a little easier." His eyelids drooped.

Had he fallen asleep? Perhaps. The sound of his ragged breathing was almost deafening in the enclosed space.

Irvana stared at the locket dangling from her fingers. It was tarnished with age and no longer than the length of her thumb. The woman it belonged to must have meant a great deal to Niklos. What had she been to him? A wife? A daughter? She'd keep it safe for as long as it took for Niklos to get well again. Irvana was about to hang it round her own neck when she noticed spatters of dark liquid on the metal. Blood.

"Ugh!"

Rosann plucked it from her hand. "I'll look after it. It'll be in me pocket 'til we get to where we're goin'."

To Irvana's relief, Rosann put the locket in her pocket, out of sight.

She must have fallen asleep at some point, because when she woke the inside of the coach was much lighter and she could hear bird song and someone crying.

Someone crying?

Still half asleep, Irvana looked at Rosann, whose

shoulders were shaking—why was Rosann crying? Then she glanced at Niklos.

His mouth was slack, his eyes fixed on nothing that was visible in this world.

The air left her lungs as though she'd been winded by a blow. Niklos was dead! Yet there was no pain, no tears. Only numbness. Irvana closed the lids over his dull eyes before leaning back in her seat and squeezing her own shut. She must not cry. If she did, she would be sure to drown in a salty flood.

And still the coach rattled on and on. Irvana's throat grew parched, her stomach growled with hunger, but she could not bear the thought of food and drink. All she wanted now was to reach Bernea.

It seemed to take forever until the bumpy road turned smoother and they were finally making good speed.

Rosann looked out of the window and described the scenery flashing past. "This road's wider than Main Street back in Koltarn, an' it's all paved, even though it's through the middle of a forest, see? Don' know what kind of trees they are, but they look like they're touchin' the sky."

The sharp scent of pine filled the coach. Irvana took a deep, cleansing breath. She'd never realised before that blood had a smell of its own.

"I can see towers, the castle's dead ahead," Rosann said, excited. "Look, Irvana. Look!"

Hadn't she seen this castle in the painting every day on the way to Aymee's room? Could it be any less forbidding to see it for real? Irvana kept her eyes fixed on her lap instead and listened to Rosann's description of the castle gates, which were apparently taller than three men and studded with great copper nails.

Finally, the coach stopped. Only then did Irvana look out of the window. They were in a large paved courtyard. A flight of stone steps led up to the castle.

Davith pulled open the coach door. "A physician will attend Niklos shortly. I sent the request ahead—" He stared at their faces and then at Niklos. He reeled back. "No!"

Tears rolled down Rosann's face. Mikal, peering over Davith's shoulder, had sparkling tracks on his cheeks. Only Irvana remained dry-eyed.

"I failed. Niklos . . ." Davith rubbed his face with his hands. "He was a good friend to my father. And to me."

Irvana tried to swallow around the tight lump in her throat. "It's not your fault. You did your best to keep us safe."

Davith grimaced, and anger flashed in his eyes. "Not safe enough."

A man in a white coat hurried down the steps of the castle and rushed towards them—the physician.

"He's of no use now," Mikal said.

Davith gripped Mikal's shoulder in a show of comfort, but Mikal shrugged him off and walked away.

Davith sighed and turned to the physician. "Niklos is beyond your help, I'm afraid." Before the man could reply, Davith looked back at the coach. "Irvana, I'm sorry, but I was ordered to find and report to the Prime Minister as soon as we arrived. Others will see to Niklos . . ."

It was true. Two men had arrived with a stretcher, to take the patient away. Only now, they would be taking a body instead. Irvana and Rosann scrambled out of the coach to allow them the space to complete their unhappy task.

"What shall I do without Niklos?" Irvana whispered. "He was going to explain everything . . ."

Davith shrugged. "You'll have to do it yourself. I know I'm a poor replacement, but . . ." He drew himself up. "I would consider it an honour if you allowed me to be present when you see Eran. I don't know all the details, but I'll willingly offer what support I can."

Irvana almost cried with relief. "Yes. Yes, please."

"Then let's go in."

They started across the courtyard.

"Mikal!" Irvana stopped and spun round. "I must talk to him before we go in, just in case . . ." She couldn't put into words the fear that she might never see him again if things went badly. She scanned the courtyard. There he was. How lost and alone he looked as he watched Niklos's body being carried gently away. She hurried over to him.

"Thank you," Irvana said. "For what you did . . . back at the palace . . . and with the bandit . . . I'm so sorry, about Niklos . . ."

Mikal's eyes were bright with tears. He nodded, as though he did not trust himself to speak.

"Keep an eye out for Rosann, won't you? She doesn't know anyone here and if . . . Eran. If . . ." She couldn't—wouldn't—say what she feared might happen, because if she did, it might come true. What more could she say to him? Just—

"Goodbye, Mikal."

As Irvana walked back to where Davith was waiting, Rosann caught her up.

"You mustn't forget this." Rosann pressed Gramma's box into Irvana's hands. "I put the locket inside, see?"

Irvana hugged the box close to her stomach.

"Ready?" Davith asked.

Irvana took a deep breath. "Ready."

Together, they walked up the steps and through the open castle doors.

CHAPTER 17
New Friends

THE BACK OF Irvana's neck prickled. She was being watched.

"They do take a bit of getting used to." Davith glanced up at the heads of deer and boar staring down at them from wall-mounted plinths. "Hunting trophies, every last one of them."

Irvana moved a little closer to Davith as they walked along the corridor. Smoking torches struggled to illuminate its darkest corners, their flickering light adding glints to the dead eyes that Irvana really wished weren't there.

They turned a corner and the corridor opened out into a huge hall. There were no heads staring at her here—just a roomful of weapons instead. Hundreds, maybe thousands, of swords and pikes were hanging on the walls, arranged in artistic displays around old-fashioned shields and metal armour. The light was reflected many times over, flashing off polished blades. Irvana didn't want to think about how much damage even one of them could inflict.

They passed through the hall and into another corridor, this one with many doors leading to who knew where? Davith opened one of them and ushered Irvana into a small room, bare except for a young man seated at a desk.

He scooted out from behind it as they entered and opened a second door. "This way."

Irvana and Davith followed him.

"Captain Davith, sir," the young man announced. Then he left, closing the door behind him.

Irvana had never seen so many books in her life. But

even they could not keep her attention when she saw the Prime Minister.

Eran straightened up from the pile of paperwork he had been bent over, and pushed his spectacles up his nose. He was a large man, with salt-and-pepper hair and a sallow-skinned face. He must have been handsome once, but a double chin had weakened his jaw and his stomach was straining the buttons of his jacket to almost bursting.

"So. The heir of Timat," he said, inspecting Irvana. "Show me the Mark."

Just like that? After everything that had happened? A wave of fatigue swept over Irvana and she swayed where she stood. Gramma's box slipped from her fingers, smashing onto the stone floor. Hands seized her before she could fall—she allowed Eran to guide her to a chair and slumped gratefully into it as Davith scooped up her grandmother's scattered memories and replaced them in their wooden sanctuary.

"Here. Drink this." Eran thrust a glass into Irvana's hand.

The liquid was sweet and cool. Irvana sipped it until her head stopped spinning.

Apparently satisfied that she was not about to faint, Eran seated himself in another chair. Unblinking brown eyes, distorted by thick circular lenses, studied her again.

"So. Evidence."

Irvana lifted the edge of her skirt and pulled at the loosely stitched hem. She took the StarRing from its hiding place and held it out.

Eran hooked the ring onto a forefinger and brought it close to his face. After a moment or two, he shook the ring off and dropped it onto a small table between their two chairs. Then he leaned back, hands folded on his stomach, his eyes hugely magnified as he stared at Irvana again.

"Where is Niklos? I thought he was coming with you?"

He didn't know what had happened. Irvana swallowed hard. "He was killed in the ambush—"

"Dead? Ambush? Explain!" The colour drained from Eran's face, leaving it wax-coloured. He leapt up.

Davith explained and for a second time, Irvana lived through the terror of the attack. This time, she felt everything she'd managed to block out. Pain, like she'd never experienced before, not even when Gramma died. Guilt, because this was all her fault. If she'd never left the shack, never gone to the city, never started working at the palace . . . And fear—of Terenz and what he was capable of. Irvana trembled. What would happen, if even after all this, Niklos was wrong?

She tightened her grip on Gramma's box and looked down, surprised. When had Davith put it in her lap?

The box was broken. There was a crack, ugly and fresh, down one corner and the lid was hanging on from a twisted hinge.

Irvana's eyes filled. She dashed the tears away and tried to push the broken sides together. It was no good. The wood split further, the contents of the box spilling out. A piece of blue fabric stuck out of the crack and Irvana tried to poke it back, but it wouldn't go. Perhaps if she pulled instead? She opened the box carefully, but there was no cloth inside to pull. So where . . . ? She didn't understand.

"Davith?"

He looked at her, and she held up the damaged box.

Davith frowned. "It's broken? We'll sort it out later." He turned back to talk to Eran.

"Not the box—look." Irvana tugged at the material sticking out of the crack. "I can't see this inside, but it's definitely there."

Davith took the box from her. He poked around inside, then tugged something. What looked like the thick base of the box came away in his hand. He'd broken it even more.

Before Irvana could protest, he handed everything back. "There's a false bottom. A secret compartment underneath. It's crude, but effective. You didn't know?"

"No. I've only looked at the things inside, I never

realised . . ." Irvana felt the narrow ridge all around the box, which the false base must have rested on. A short leather cord was attached to the base—was that what Davith had used to pull it free?

The blue fabric had been hidden—but why?

It looked like a scrap of blanket. Irvana rubbed the softness between her fingers and felt something else—something hard, wrapped inside. She pulled the fabric aside, eager to see what it was, and uncovered a large golden disc on a heavy chain. Hardly daring to breathe, she lifted it up. The disc dangled from her fingers, rotating slowly. Engraved on one side was a seven-pointed star, its diamond-studded rays sending rainbows dancing across the books on the walls. On the other side was a detailed picture of what was, unmistakeably, the cliffs of Koltarn.

"The StarChain!" Davith gasped.

What? Irvana looked up.

Davith's face was lit up with joy. Eran's mouth opened and closed, but nothing came out of it.

Irvana's fingers tingled and felt as though they were burning. She dropped the StarChain, if that's what it was, on the table, next to the StarRing.

"So Timat did take it with him . . ." Eran dropped heavily into his seat. "The woman you thought was your grandmother must have stolen it when she took the ring."

The accusation stung. "Maybe she didn't know what it was—"

Eran shook his head. "No one who came from Koltarn could fail to recognise the sacred star. Her action had to be a deliberate one. Thank heavens it's been recovered."

"Terenz's position can be validated," Davith said. "There will be a golden star for Koltarn again."

Eran shot Davith a look. "Perhaps. There are many who desire such an outcome." He paused to polish his spectacles. "But there is a complication . . ." He put the glasses back on and leaned forward in his chair. "There are apparently two StarMarks. May I see?"

This was the moment. Irvana bent her head and tried not to pull away as clammy fingers probed the skin under her plait.

"Thank you. The Mark appears to be genuine, as far as I can tell."

Irvana's brain whirled.

Eran stood. "This is a delicate situation. Only one Mark can be gold. If you are truly Timat's daughter, as Niklos suspected, then Terenz faces the prospect of losing the overlordship." He cleared his throat. "I will order the immediate reconvening of the Council, though it may be some time before all the members are able to return to Bernea. There must be a formal presentation to them, of both yourself and the StarChain, as it would be disastrous for a Mark to become golden without the change being witnessed. The Council could accuse us of falsification, you see. There have been tales . . . of stars tattooed into flesh, or finely wrought gold stitched to skin."

Would men really go to such desperate lengths for power? Irvana felt the back of her neck and bit her lip, trying not to think of how painful a tattooist's needle would be.

"I suggest that we keep the discovery of the StarChain between the three of us for the time being," Eran continued. "I will take responsibility for it and the StarRing, as there are some who would be eager for Terenz to benefit from the StarChain's rediscovery, rather than give you, Irvana, a chance to prove your own position. Captain Davith, I think it would be wise, under the circumstances, to appoint you as Irvana's protector until this matter can be resolved. We cannot afford any attempt on her life."

An emotion flickered across Davith's face that Irvana did not recognise. Eran walked to the door and pulled on a thick rope hanging beside it. Moments later, the door opened and a lady walked in. She wasn't tall or particularly beautiful, but her elegant dress and the jewels around her throat indicated that this was no housekeeper. Her face was filled with concern as she walked straight to Irvana.

"You poor dear," she murmured.

Irvana's bottom lip wobbled. She managed a weak smile, but did not trust herself to speak.

"Come. Bed, I think." The lady drew Irvana to her feet and placed a supporting arm around her waist.

Eran stepped forward. "I have not relayed all your instructions—"

"I do not need instruction on how to look after a distressed child," the lady retorted sharply. "Anything more than that can wait until the morning."

The lady led Irvana out of the book-filled chamber, along a maze of corridors, and finally into a suite of rooms. With every step Irvana took, her exhaustion grew, until it was all she could do to place one foot in front of the other. She barely registered being in a bedroom, where the lady helped her to undress, before Irvana climbed into the bed. How heavy her bones felt. Her eyelids drooped and it took far too much effort to keep them open. As she sank into the soft mattress, she was dimly aware of stray hairs being brushed from her cheek.

"Poor child," the lady whispered. "Sleep well."

And she did.

Irvana woke to sun coming in through the window and new surroundings. Snuggled between crisp white sheets, she looked around the room. How different it all was to the servant's quarters at the palace.

She saw Gramma's box, sitting in front of a small mirror on a dressing table. Another, larger mirror, stood in the corner, near a wardrobe with beautiful birds painted on its doors. Heavy damask curtains hung on either side of a narrow window.

And there were clothes, draped over a chair. Irvana pushed the covers aside and crept to the foot of the bed for a closer look.

"For me?" she whispered.

There were undergarments made of soft linen and whiter than any cloud. Gone was yesterday's patched dress; in its place lay a gown of blue satin and a pair of silk slippers. Irvana dressed quickly, the silk whispering over the linen and settling against her skin, cool and smooth to the touch. Then she pushed her feet into the shoes. Whoever had chosen the clothes had guessed well at her size—they were a good fit.

Irvana used the silver-backed brush on the dressing table to rid her hair of tangles. She laid the brush down, and Gramma's box caught her eye, reminding her about the locket. She emptied everything out of the box, laid Gramma's memories in a line, and picked up what Niklos had given her. He'd worn it on a chain, but there was a clasp on the back so it could be worn as a brooch instead.

Using the scrap of blue fabric, Irvana rubbed away Niklos's dried blood and polished the silver. Poor Niklos. He'd tried so hard to protect her. But she didn't want to remember him dying in the carriage . . . She concentrated on her task, not stopping until the locket shone. It was decorated with curls and flourishes, with something in the middle that almost looked like entwined letters. Was there anything inside, she wondered. Perhaps the identity of the woman Niklos had spoken of?

Irvana tried to prise the locket open, but it remained shut. She gave up, pulled the locket from the chain, and pinned it to her dress. It seemed right to wear it in memory of Niklos. Then she took her courage in both hands and opened the bedroom door.

She vaguely remembered passing through the empty sitting room when she had arrived—now it was occupied.

In an overstuffed armchair beside a white marble fireplace was a sandy-haired man. He was reading a book and spirals of pipe smoke curled around his head while he stroked a large dog sitting by his chair. A portrait of a red-headed girl, hanging over the fireplace, smiled down at him.

"My dear, Irvana, you are awake at last." The lady from the previous evening put her embroidery to one side and left her window seat, arms open in welcome as she approached Irvana. "We thought it best to leave you to sleep after the rigours of your journey. How do you feel?"

"Very well, thank you, my lady." Irvana bobbed a curtsey.

"Please, there's no need for us to stand on ceremony. You are a guest in our home." The lady smiled. "You must call me Faye. This is my husband, Lenad." Faye held her hand out to the gentleman who was watching Irvana over the top of his book. The dog thumped its tail against the floor a couple of times then settled at Lenad's feet and dropped his nose onto his paws.

"Oh! Mikal's going to be your page," Irvana said.

Lenad pulled at the thin strip of sandy beard growing down the middle of his chin, and his eyes crinkled as he smiled. "He is. I believe you brought that rascal with you?"

Irvana nodded. "I'm not sure where he is at the moment, though."

Lenad chuckled. "Oh, he'll turn up I expect. Just like a bad penny."

"In the meantime, we are charged with looking after you, until such time as Eran decides differently," Faye said. "Our apartment is not the most splendid here, but I hope that you will be comfortable. You will, I'm afraid, be confined to these rooms and limited to our company until the presentation. Captain Davith will visit—"

"And Mikal will be around as well," Lenad said, "though he won't get much chance to chat. I've a mind to keep the young scamp as busy as I can."

"You must tell us if you need anything," Faye continued, "and we will do our best to supply it."

"Thank you."

Irvana was safe and in good hands. For the first time in several days, she relaxed. What more could she possibly need? Her stomach rumbled loudly—it had been a long time since she'd eaten properly.

Faye ignored Irvana's embarrassment and pulled on a bell rope. She gave instructions to the servant who appeared at the door and not too long after, Irvana was at a table eating a plateful of eggs and bacon, with several thick slices of bread dripping with honey to follow.

While Irvana ate, she studied the room. It was eight-sided in shape, and she guessed they must be in one of the towers. Three of the walls had doors set in them. One led to the room she'd slept in, another she thought must be Faye and Lenad's bedroom, and the third was where the servant and food came through—presumably it went back into the castle. Three more walls were filled with large windows overlooking the pine forest. The fireplace took up the seventh wall, and the eighth was covered, floor to ceiling, with shelves full of books. The furniture looked careworn, as though it was much loved and often used, and hand-stitched cushions and slightly shabby tufted rugs added to the feeling of homeliness.

With her stomach pleasantly full, Irvana licked the stickiness from her fingers.

Faye put aside her sewing. "Irvana, the brooch you are wearing. Where did it come from?"

"Niklos." Irvana traced the edges of the locket. "He was wearing it when he was attacked, gave it to me before he died. I think it must have belonged to someone he loved very much."

"Niklos?" Faye sounded doubtful. "May I see?"

Irvana unpinned the locket and gave it to her.

Faye paled. "I thought it was," she whispered hoarsely. "Lenad . . ."

Lenad unfolded himself from his chair and peered over Faye's shoulder.

"See? The A and T joined together. It is hers, isn't it?" Faye searched Lenad's face.

Lenad nodded and looked grave.

"Whose?" Irvana whispered.

"Have you looked inside it?" Lenad asked.

"No, I couldn't open it."

Lenad and Faye exchanged a glance. Lenad took the locket and coaxed the two halves open. Then he handed it back to Irvana.

She held it gently, her hands shaking. Why was she suddenly so afraid? She lowered her eyes to look.

There were two tiny exquisite portraits inside. One in each door, the painted colours still bright. Irvana did not recognise the beautiful young woman whose dark eyes looked out at the world with such intensity, but she knew the man.

Timat's star was a miniscule golden dot on his hand.

"Lord Timat," Faye said. "And his princess, the Lady Ailsa. This was his wedding present to her. I don't remember her ever being without it. My dear child, if what is suspected is true, then these are your parents."

Tears sprang into Irvana's eyes, blurring the tiny paintings. She blinked them away and studied the miniature portraits closely, searching the faces for any similarities to her own. Were her eyes like her father's? Difficult to tell on such a small scale. She knew her mouth was wide—like her mother's—and her hair was much darker than Timat's, with no trace of Ailsa's copper.

Irvana looked up. "If it was Ailsa's, why did Niklos have it?"

Faye laid a hand over Irvana's. "You must understand, his sole purpose in life was to serve the StarMarks of Koltarn. Niklos served both Terenz and Timat, and their father before them. He was devoted to his job and never had a family of his own. I think he viewed Timat as an adopted son and when Ailsa became part of the StarMark dynasty, he treated her like a daughter. It was obvious to us all that he loved them both very much, was devastated by their deaths.

No wonder he did everything he could to protect you when he realised who you were."

"But look what happened to him." The weight of guilt and remorse would crush her, she was sure of it. She snatched her hand from under Faye's and dug her nails into her palms, fighting to hold back more tears. "If Terenz hadn't found out . . ."

Faye took Irvana's hand again. "We are both just as willing to protect you," she said, with tears sparkling in her own eyes.

Irvana cried then. Between sobs, she told Faye and Lenad everything—the shock of Gramma dying, the journey to Koltarn, how Matteuw had refused to help, how she thought she'd be safe at the palace and how Terenz had discovered her Mark and tried to erase the evidence. She told them how Mikal and Niklos had helped her escape, why Rosann had been forced to come with them, and how Captain Davith had brought them to Bernea.

Eventually, Irvana hiccupped herself into silence.

Faye put an arm around her. "You've been through so much, been so brave. But we're here, and we'll help as much as we're able to."

"We can't change the past, though I wish we could," Lenad said. "But we can help with the here and now. I think you need a friend of your own age while this matter is being resolved. And I think I know who that should be." He ordered a pallet bed to be brought to Irvana's room and when it arrived, so did Rosann.

"Rosann!" Irvana jumped up and seized her in a tight hug.

Rosann disentangled herself and fought to get her breath back. "I'm not so sure about this mesel', if you're goin' to squeeze the life out o' me whenever I've bin gone more than five minutes," she grumbled, but her eyes sparkled. "Well, look at you. You're turnin' into a lady already."

Irvana pulled at her silk skirt. "It's not mine. I'm borrowing it, but I'm not sure who from."

Pain flashed across Faye's face and Lenad took her hand.

"The dress belonged to our daughter," Faye said quietly, her eyes drawn to the portrait above the fireplace. "Katrin died when she was only a little older than you are now. We kept her room, yours whilst you are here, just as it was . . ."

"Oh!" She was wearing a dead girl's dress? Irvana bit her lip, ashamed of how thoughtless her remark must have sounded. Was she able to do anything that didn't cause pain to those around her? "I don't have to wear it, I don't mind wearing my old clothes—"

"Nonsense, my dear." Faye forced a smile. "Katrin would have been glad to know that the dress is finally getting some use after so many years shut up in the wardrobe. There are others too. I . . . *we* . . . should be delighted to think they are being brought back to life. Come, let me show you."

She took Irvana and Rosann into the bedroom and flung the wardrobe doors open.

Inside were more dresses than Irvana could imagine one person ever needing. "Are these what the ladies at court wear?" She dared to trace the delicate leaf embroidery on a skirt of lime green satin.

"They're a little outdated. Katrin has been gone for ten years," Faye said. "Nevertheless, you will still be able to hold your head high when wearing any one of them."

Rosann pulled out a mass of ruby silk, decorated with swirls of silver. "Look at this."

"Try it on," Faye said. "But first . . ." She quickly sorted through the rest of the dresses and held them against Irvana. She discarded some of them and threw them onto the bed, others she loaded into Rosann's arms until Rosann almost disappeared under a multi-coloured mountain of material.

Irvana put the red dress on and looked at herself in the mirror. A stranger stared back at her, a stranger whose lips were almost the same colour as the silk and for whom the silver swirls highlighted the grey flecks in her eyes.

"Beautiful. Now try the deep blue."

Irvana stepped out of the first dress and into the second. On and on went the succession of dresses until there were a good dozen found which fitted. Faye finally gave her approval to the last dress, and Irvana sank to the floor, exhausted, her yellow skirt spread around her like a pool of molten gold.

Life in Bernea was certainly going to be different.

CHAPTER 18
Waiting

IRVANA WAS SAFE in Bernea, but for how long? The shadow of the StarMark hung over her head like a guillotine, ready to crash down at any moment.

Confined as she was to Faye and Lenad's apartment, she felt as though she was in jail. It was a comfortable jail, true, and one where her jailers almost overwhelmed her with kindness, where her friends came and went freely . . . But her friends were changing . . .

The former veg girl was learning the role of a lady's maid. Faye did not approve of the easy banter that Irvana and Rosann had always shared, so Irvana had to be careful of what she said. Mikal had begun his training too—his new duties often brought him to the cosy rooms. But when they did, he appeared uncomfortable in Irvana's presence. Was it the memory of Niklos's death that made him feel that way, or the fact that she might actually be the rightful overlord of Koltarn?

Either way, Irvana felt as though her friends were drifting away from her. She was out of place here and would remain so until the presentation, when the truth of the matter would be revealed beyond doubt.

"Will I ever fit in here, even if my Mark does change?" she whispered to her reflection in the mirror.

Davith came to see her often. He offered a glimpse of life beyond the rooms Irvana was trapped in, telling her of drills and duties and listing the members of the Council who had already returned. Sometimes, he would set aside his helmet and sword and lay out the Tacala board, perhaps sensing Irvana's frustration and allowing her to take it out on the game. Under his direction, Irvana improved and became an excellent player.

"A worthy opponent indeed," he said, the day she finally beat him.

Even with Tacala, the days still dragged as Irvana waited. Until, that is, Davith took her to see the master of arms.

"Eran wants to be prepared," Davith told her as he escorted her through the castle. "If your Mark turns, he intends to unveil your coat of arms immediately after."

A knot of apprehension tightened in Irvana's chest as she hurried alongside Davith. There was that word again. If.

They arrived in the master's room, and it was empty.

"Manek's not here? He's rather absent minded—I bet he's forgotten." Davith flashed a smile at Irvana. "You wait here. I'll go and find him."

This room was the first new place Irvana had been in for days and she looked round with interest. Huge wingback chairs sat on either side of the fireplace, positioned with their backs to the door to protect whoever sat in them from draughts. A large table stood by the window, laid with a precise arrangement of books, paint pots, and brushes. Irvana was drawn towards the table, intrigued by the neat piles of loose parchment sheets. Leafing through, she saw that each sheet showed a different coat of arms. They were in various stages of completion, some still pencil sketches, others filled in with vibrant colours. She pulled one of them from the pile to take a closer look—a white shield with a black seven-pointed star at its centre.

"I have an idea for a new blazon actually."

Irvana swung around with a gasp.

Terenz was unfolding his long body from where he'd been sitting in one of the wingback chairs.

Irvana couldn't move, couldn't speak. What was he going to do? Would anyone hear if she screamed?

Terenz was all black and white like his shield as he strode towards her. No, that wasn't quite true—there was a flash of silver on his finger and the fresh scar on his cheek was vivid red. He snatched the parchment from Irvana, his face taut and white with fury.

"Let me show you." He flung the parchment down on the table, grabbed a brush, and plunged it into a pot of red paint. His jaw clenched tight as he drew a vicious stroke across the page. "See? A diagonal line, right through the star. Much truer to life, don't you think, beet girl? To commemorate the addition to my Mark." He thrust the sheet back into her hand.

Irvana looked down at the parchment. The paint had run and it looked as though, like Terenz's cheek, the paper had been slashed and was bleeding. She dropped the sheet onto the table, trying to shake the image of Terenz, lying bleeding in the middle of Mikal's carpet, from her head.

"Some time ago, I received a message with unbelievable news," Terenz said.

From his pocket, he drew out a smaller piece of crumpled parchment and with exaggerated care, smoothed out its creases. He leaned across Irvana to lay it beside the altered shield and his arm brushed her shoulder.

A shock ran through Irvana's body at his closeness, but she couldn't move away.

Terenz pointed at the note.

Irvana couldn't read it, but at the bottom, where she supposed a signature would normally be, there was a blob of black wax stamped with a symbol—a tiny star set alongside a "T."

"Failed to stop Timat's heir reaching Bernea," Terenz read, his finger underlining the words as he spoke. "Evidence of paternity already presented. StarChain rediscovered. Long live the Black Star."

Irvana reeled as if struck by lightning. Terenz knew about the StarChain? How? Had Eran told him, in spite of his insistence that the discovery be kept secret? And that phrase—long live the black star—it meant someone else knew, someone who had tried hard to stop Irvana from reaching Bernea.

Terenz snatched up the note, and Irvana flinched, her heart pounding in her chest. Where was Davith? She needed him—now!

But Terenz did not attack, as she feared. He went to stand by the fireplace and watched her with a hungry expression in his eyes. "I had suspected that I was an uncle prior to the receipt of this message. I had no idea about the StarChain though. If I'd realised that it was in your possession sooner . . ." Terenz traced the jagged line on his cheek. "And now the Council has been recalled, because Eran thinks this is the most compelling claim for the StarMark we have had for years. Do you know, he insisted I should have no dealings with you until the presentation? I can't imagine why."

Irvana could.

"If you are unsuccessful in your claim, I envisage a second ceremony taking place rather rapidly afterwards, to verify my own. Then, at last, I shall obtain a golden star." Terenz's grey eyes glittered with naked greed. Then he blinked and his voice lost its edge. "But we should think of less weighty matters in the meantime. There can be only one reason why you are here, to create your shield, should you need it. What will be on your coat of arms I wonder? A beetroot?" His voice dripped with sarcasm.

The door opened.

Davith walked in, closely followed by a stranger, a man whose left side twitched violently as soon as he spotted Terenz. Davith tensed and dropped his hand onto his sword. For a long moment he froze, eyes flicking between Irvana and Terenz, then he swiftly crossed the room to her.

"Are you alright?" he asked, keeping his voice low.

Irvana managed a nod.

"My Lord. I was n-n-not expecting you," the stranger stammered, wringing his hands.

"I came to discuss a change to my shield, Manek." Terenz indicated the altered original on the table, exposing his injured cheek as he did so.

Davith drew in his breath sharply. "Your Mark. My Lord, what happened?"

"An accident," Terenz replied easily, though his jaw clenched. "It is of no consequence."

Manek was distracted by the wet brush lying on the floor and the dribbles of red paint splashed over the otherwise pristine work surface. His body twitched again and he clasped his hands together, stilling them. "A new blazon. I shall see that it is registered . . . ah . . . if required, my Lord."

"Do so." Terenz smiled. "Captain Davith. I thought your family were supporters of the StarMark dynasty?" His voice was like silk, but the words were full of poison.

Davith stood to attention, his face an unreadable mask. "My family have been and will remain loyal to that dynasty, my Lord."

"Is that so?" Terenz stopped smiling and scowled. "Then how do you explain your presence here? With the beet girl?"

Davith shot Irvana a look, and her cheeks grew warm.

"I repeat, my loyalty is to the dynasty," Davith said. "Not to an individual. At present, I am merely performing the duty laid upon me by the Prime Minister, to protect the future of the StarMarks of Koltarn."

Terenz grunted. "And what of protecting my future? Your allegiance appears to have switched very easily to the newcomer. Perhaps you are not the man of integrity I thought you were."

Davith's nostrils flared, but he kept silent.

Terenz turned to Irvana. "I doubt we shall be allowed to talk again before your presentation, beet girl. Until that time . . ." He sneered and performed an elaborate bow.

Irvana's knees gave a jerky response as they tried to make her curtsey. Without acknowledging either Davith or Manek, Terenz took his leave, and slammed the door behind him.

Muscle by muscle, Irvana unfroze and found she could breathe again.

Davith stared at her. "I am so sorry. I would never have left you alone if I'd thought for one moment—"

"But nothing happened. It's alright." Irvana laid a hand on his arm. Under her fingers his muscles were knotted. He was as taut as a strung bow. Davith blew out a deep breath and she felt some of the tension seep away.

"It will not happen again. I will stand guard outside and prevent any further intrusions." Davith spun on his heel, marched quickly to the door, and closed it behind him without a sound.

Manek muttered to himself, ignoring Irvana. He set the parchment Terenz had defaced aside to dry, mopped up the blobs and smudges caused by Terenz's overzealous brushstrokes, and reorganised the paint pots, affecting tiny adjustments to their ordered positions. He was finally satisfied with their arrangement and looked up at Irvana.

"Ah . . . so . . . the Prime Minister requires me to design a shield for you, in case of the . . . ah . . . happy circumstance that you are blessed with a golden Mark." The words were accompanied with a twitch. "Every overlord has a distinctive crest, though only those belonging to the . . . ah . . . overlords of Koltarn include a golden star. Of course . . . ah . . . that is absent in the case of Lord Terenz." Again the nervous twitch—more violent it seemed because of the mention of Terenz's name. "His suggestion for an amendment is not strictly speaking correct in heraldic terms, but what Lord Terenz wants, he usually gets."

Irvana did not want to think about what that might mean for her. "Do you draw them all? Can I see some?" she asked, keen to steer the subject away from Terenz.

"Oh yes, indeed." Manek selected a large book from a stack on the tabletop and opened it at random. "This is the register for Koltarn. See—"

Pages and pages of brightly coloured shields flashed past Irvana's eyes. Suddenly, she put out her hand to stop Manek from turning the page.

"Ah. Argent on a sinister hand gules couped appaumé a mullet of seven or," Manek said.

"A what?"

Manek glanced at her. "Forgive me. I forget that not everyone speaks the language of heraldry. For the uninitiated—"

Why did that feel like a criticism?

"—a golden star on a red hand, resting on a white shield. Lord Timat's blazon."

Irvana thought of the laughing man in the portrait. How appropriate that his shield should show so literally where his star had been. And his was only one of many—this book of shields represented many generations who had borne the StarMark. If her own was proved to be genuine, she would be following in the footsteps of all who had gone before.

Right at this moment, she felt woefully unprepared.

Manek closed the book with a bang. "It is your design we must consider, not those which already exist. What shall it be? A bird . . . ah . . . rising in flight with a star in its beak, to indicate the discovery of a long lost heir?"

"That sounds rather grand," Irvana said. "Isn't there something simpler we can use?"

"Like what?"

"Um . . ." Irvana racked her brains. "Could it be something to do with the sea? I grew up on the coast with my . . . I grew up on the coast."

Manek's eyes glazed over while he thought. "Hmmm . . . blue sea . . . a journey . . . of course."

He drew a fresh piece of parchment from the pile, selected a sharpened pencil, and set to work. As he sketched out the design and added colour, he explained the meaning of the various parts. "The base is blue, for the sea. The shell is cream, represents pilgrimage, which is a journey both literally and metaphorically. And of course the golden star—within the shell, I think."

Irvana watched as the picture came to life in Manek's expert hands.

"Done. Azure on an escallop proper a mullet of seven or." Manek laid down his brush. "A seven pointed gold star on a shell overlaid on a blue background."

"It's beautiful." Irvana picked the parchment up, careful not to smudge the still-wet paint.

"Keep that one. I'll draw up a precise copy for the records . . . ah . . . if, of course, it is ever registered." The twitch, which had disappeared while Manek concentrated on his artwork, returned with a vengeance.

A knock at the door announced Davith's return. "Eran wants to see you."

All the way to the Prime Minister's office, Irvana worried. Why had Eran summoned her? Had she broken some unwritten code of conduct? Had someone seen her and guessed at the reason for her presence in Bernea? Surely Eran hadn't already found out about the unplanned meeting with Terenz? That wasn't her fault . . .

They arrived at the office and found Eran seated behind a wide desk. Irvana fidgeted nervously on the edge of a chair in front of the desk, and Davith took up his position by her side.

"Every member of the Council has returned to Bernea. There is no reason to delay." Eran peered at Irvana through his spectacles. "The presentation will be tomorrow. You will be required to state your case, in person, and we shall finally discover the truth. If your claim is true, Terenz will have to step aside. He'll have lost the overlordship, but gained a niece. If it is false . . ."

Goosebumps rippled down Irvana's arms. If it was false . . . "What will happen then?" she whispered.

Eran frowned. "Let us face that possibility only if we need to."

But what *would* they do with her? She'd find out soon enough. Less than a day until . . . Irvana couldn't face either the possibility that she was the rightful overlord of Koltarn, or that she wasn't, yet she couldn't stop thinking about it all the way back to Faye and Lenad's apartments.

"I'll see you later," Davith said as he saw her inside.

There was surprise waiting for her in the sitting room— Mikal, lounging in Lenad's favourite chair. He almost fell out of the chair when he saw Irvana.

"What are you doing here?" Irvana couldn't help grinning at his guilty expression. Lenad usually kept his page busy, but it looked as though Mikal had wangled a rare opportunity to be idle and was making the most of it.

"Lenad's gone off to see Eran, didn't need me so he said I could wait here."

"And Faye couldn't find anything for you to do either?" Irvana was enjoying making him squirm.

"No. She took Rosann off to find ribbon or something. When they'd gone, I made myself comfy."

"I can see that. Does that mean I've got you to myself for a while?" Irvana tried not to sound too pleased.

"I'm not doing anything for you, either," Mikal snapped.

"I wasn't going to ask. I just want to talk. Please?"

Mikal relaxed back into the chair. "Alright. Did you know the presentation's tomorrow?"

What a subject to begin with. "Yes," Irvana said and shivered.

Mikal tutted. "You're not worried, are you? You've got a StarMark—what could go wrong? You'll be overlord of Koltarn before you can say 'StarRing'!"

"I don't want to talk about that. Look, can we play Tacala instead?" Irvana began to set up the counters.

"If we must." Mikal reluctantly threw the dice for his first move. "What if your Mark doesn't change, though?"

Irvana moved her own counter, wishing she'd never

started this. "D'you think they'll carry on keeping me a prisoner?"

"You're not a prisoner." Mikal frowned and moved his counter sideways two spaces.

"Not a prisoner? What do you call it, then, when you're confined to certain rooms and can't go out without a soldier by your side?" Suddenly angry, Irvana jumped to her feet. "You have no idea what it's like. I've waited and worried, terrified of what Terenz will do if my Mark isn't real, and petrified that I won't live up to everybody's expectations if it is. And I've been shut inside with the same people day in, day out. I want it all to be over." She slammed a fist onto the table, making the remaining counters jump off their places.

"I didn't realise you felt like that." Mikal looked uncomfortable.

"Well, I do." Irvana's anger fizzled away as quickly as it had come, leaving her drained. She let out her breath in a deep sigh. "I'm sorry. It's not fair to take it out on you." She turned away from him, went to one of the windows, and rested her forehead against the glass. "I just wish I could go outside."

"Why don't you?"

"I'm not allowed. Eran said—"

"Blow what Eran said." Mikal came to stand beside her. "He won't find out. We can go now, while Faye and Rosann are finding ribbons. We'll be back before anyone misses us."

It was so tempting . . . Irvana could feel herself weakening. "Are you sure?"

Mikal nodded.

"Oh, just for a little while then." She couldn't stop grinning as she followed Mikal out of the apartment, along the corridor, and down a narrow winding staircase.

At the bottom of the stairs, Irvana stepped through a door into an enclosed garden. It was small and square, with an ivy-clad urn in each of the four corners. Climbing roses were growing up a trellis on the walls, their perfume overwhelmingly strong in the warm sunlight and small space. There was a handkerchief-sized lawn, and in the middle of that was a bronze statue, green with age, showing some mythical creature writhing at the feet of a victorious hunter.

Irvana kicked off her shoes. She had grass under her feet for the first time in months. How good it felt! She danced and twirled until, laughing and dizzy, she staggered towards Mikal. He was leaning against one of the urns, looking mightily pleased with himself.

"Glad you came?"

"Oh, yes! The roses smell gorgeous." Irvana took a huge sniff of the nearest one before snapping its stem and pushing the flower into her hair.

"Irvana!"

She and Mikal jumped.

Davith and another soldier were striding towards them. "What are you doing? You know you must not leave the rooms without an escort. Faye came back, found you missing, and raised the alarm. I've half the guard out looking for you."

Irvana had never seen Davith so angry—his knuckles were white where he gripped the hilt of his sword, his face thunderous.

"Mikal persuaded me—"

"I wanted to take her mind off—" Mikal said at the same time.

Davith glared at them.

"Sergeant, go back to Lady Faye. Assure her that all is well and we will all be returning shortly."

The sergeant ran out of the garden. Irvana wished she could do the same.

"What on earth were you thinking, you stupid boy?" Davith said, his voice tight with anger. "Do you ever actually think of the consequences of your actions? No wonder Lord Terenz wanted you to learn some responsibility. I've a good mind to—"

"It's not all his fault," Irvana said, unwilling to let Mikal take the blame. "I knew I shouldn't, but I wanted to come out. There's no harm done."

"No harm done!" Davith exploded, sending a couple of pigeons flying off from their roost at the top of the wall. "You've already had one close shave today with Terenz. What if coming into the garden had provided him with another chance to get close to you? To destroy his opposition?"

Irvana gasped.

"It's my job to ensure the safety of the StarMark. No one knew where you'd gone and if anything had happened—"

"But it didn't," Irvana whispered, avoiding Davith's furious expression by inspecting her toes. "I just wanted to come outside, I've been cooped up for so long . . . I'm sorry, really I am."

Davith blew out a long breath.

Irvana looked up, saw his face had relaxed a little, though it was still dreadfully stern.

"We are too close to the presentation to risk anything going wrong now. You may stay a little longer. I will be waiting at the bottom of the staircase to take you back. After that, there will be no more trips out. Understand? Mikal? You too?" He marched to the door that led to the staircase.

Irvana daren't look at Mikal as she slipped her feet back into her shoes. How could she have been so stupid? How must Faye have felt, coming back to the empty rooms? Of course that good lady would have feared the worst, especially knowing that if the presentation was going ahead, Terenz must be somewhere in the castle. All this upset and upheaval, just for a few selfish moments outside. She was so ashamed of herself.

"I shouldn't have suggested it." Mikal looked as wretched as Irvana felt.

"I'm just as much to blame. Why can't life be how we want it to be?" Irvana brushed away a tear. "Mikal, are we still going to be friends, once tomorrow's over?"

"We don't know what's going to happen," Mikal said, his voice shaking a little. "I can't say . . . I . . ."

Irvana felt as if a thick cloud had appeared from nowhere, blotting out the sun. She shivered. If Niklos was wrong, if she was just a girl with a strange birthmark, would she lose everything—even her friends?

She had never felt so alone.

"We should be getting back," she said and in miserable silence, walked back inside.

CHAPTER 19
The Presentation

IT WAS ALMOST time.

"This anteroom is usually used to hold high profile prisoners before they enter the Council Chamber for their trials," Faye told Irvana. "Room enough for a couple of armed guards and a man in chains . . ."

Irvana felt the blood drain from her face and even after Faye's hurried reassurances, she couldn't stop thinking that the presentation *was* a trial, of sorts. Oh, she wasn't a criminal—but she might certainly be viewed as an imposter. She suppressed a shiver of unease at the sound of men's voices in the room next door.

Rosann jumped to her feet. "Was that the bell?"

"Rosann. Will you sit still? That's the fourth time you've made me prick myself." Faye sucked her bleeding finger while Rosann apologised. "No matter." She sighed, laying aside her needlework. "I've not managed half a dozen stitches this morning—I'll try again later."

Would it have been better to have waited alone? Irvana picked at the embroidery on her skirt. At least that way she'd only have had her own nerves to contend with.

The door from the Council Chamber opened, the voices swelling until Davith closed the door behind him and the sound of the assembled men settled to a muted rumble.

"They are ready." His face was serious. "Eran will ring the bell at the given time and I will escort you in, as arranged."

Irvana's stomach did a complete somersault and churned unpleasantly. She'd been both wanting and dreading this moment in equal measure. In just a few moments time, they would know for sure whether or not she was really Timat's daughter.

The bell rang, and Irvana flinched, even though she had been expecting it.

"This is it." Davith opened the door. "A golden star for Koltarn, after all these years."

Feeling as though she were dreaming, Irvana stood. But she couldn't move. The bell rang a second time and she finally took the first step towards her future.

She entered the Council Chamber. To her left, the room stretched away towards double doors underneath a gilded balcony. To her right was the raised platform where she knew the Prime Minister would be waiting. She walked in that direction, even though every instinct was telling her to run the other way. She faltered in her step as she stared at the sea of men's faces turned towards her, most of them scowling. A few had raised eyebrows, puzzled at her presence in this male domain.

The only smile of welcome was Lenad's.

Irvana would not let them intimidate her. Thankful for the long skirt which hid her shaking legs, she lifted her chin and moved as confidently as she could through the silent men, conscious of Davith keeping pace with her.

High above their heads, narrow windows let bright sunlight fall on hundreds of banners suspended from the ceiling, striping the tiled floor with shadows. A good number of the banners bore the golden star of Koltarn and Irvana spotted Timat's red hand. But the thrill she felt on recognising it disappeared when she saw the black star hanging beside it.

She drew closer to the platform. Eran was standing beside a small table, where she knew the evidence of her alleged birthright rested on a silver tray. She could tell nothing of how Eran felt about this moment. His face was set, unreadable. At the foot of the steps, Davith stopped, leaving Irvana to climb onto the platform alone.

"The Council have been recalled to bear witness to . . ." Eran began.

Irvana didn't hear the rest of what he said. Her eyes met those of Lord Terenz, who was also on the platform, and she couldn't look away.

He radiated confidence and authority, looking every inch the overlord. He had chosen to wear the jacket which Irvana remembered Andela giving him on his birthday and the light flashed on the silver stars around his wrist as he tugged at the cuff of a blood red shirt.

What must she look like, standing next to him? A frightened child? She knew it must have been true because the corners of Terenz's mouth twitched and settled into the smile of a predator. Still watching her, he hooked his hair behind his ear, baring his Mark for all to see. The scar had faded as it healed, but the star on his cheek was distorted; a permanent reminder of what had happened in Koltarn.

Irvana looked away first. There was no way she could stand up to the unspoken challenge in those steely grey eyes.

At the other end of the room, she saw a movement on the gilded balcony. Was that a blonde head of someone peering down through a gap in the hanging banners? Mikal? But he wasn't supposed to be here—Lenad had been very firm on that point.

If it was Mikal, it meant that everyone she considered a friend—Faye, Lenad, Davith, Rosann and now Mikal—were close.

"—therefore required to hear the evidence in support of this claim."

The tail end of Eran's speech. Irvana dragged her attention back to what she should be doing.

"Do you swear to answer in truth before this Council?" Eran asked.

Irvana's lips were dry. She ran her tongue over them. "I do."

"Then explain, please, the circumstances that lead you to believe you could be the daughter of the deceased Lord Timat."

This was it. Trying to ignore the many faces staring up at her, fighting the impulse to run, Irvana began to speak. Hesitantly at first, and then with growing confidence. She told them the simple facts. How she had come to be in the palace, how Gramma's box had given up its secret treasure, and how Niklos had been the one to realise what it all might mean.

Eran indicated the table beside him with a sweeping gesture. "I can confirm that the items recovered from the box, displayed here, did indeed belong to Lord Timat. The StarChain, thought to be lost for so many years, lends weight to the authenticity of this discovery. I can also confirm the presence of what appears to be a StarMark." He gave the signal.

With a start, Irvana remembered what she had to do. She turned her back on the men and lifted up her plait. Fierce whispering broke out behind her on the chamber floor and she risked another glance at Terenz. He'd stopped smiling— his mouth was now a thin tight line. A muscle twitched in his jaw as he stared at the banner with the black star.

"The evidence regarding the girl's paternity is compelling." Eran's voice broke through the whispering. "But the true test is to ascertain whether the Mark is genuine. With the StarChain happily returned to us, I propose a challenge. If Irvana is truly who she claims to be, her StarMark will turn." He lifted the StarChain from the tray. The diamond points of the star reflected the light, sending rainbows shooting across the faces of the Council in a merry dance.

So beautiful, Irvana thought.

A heavy jolt ran through her body, almost as though she'd been struck by a mighty hand. She looked down. Protruding from her chest was a short wooden shaft with black feathers quivering at its end. Where the shaft disappeared into her flesh, her dress was turning red.

Irvana felt nothing, except confusion.

"Let the claim be tested—" Eran began, but his voice faltered and died.

In the silence which followed, sensation flooded back. Pain—hot, searing pain—shot through Irvana's chest. She struggled to lift her head up, but managed to raise it enough to see the Eran's horrified face.

"Oh!" she said. Then her knees buckled and the room went black.

CHAPTER 20
Betrayal

WHEN HE HEARD the shouting, Mikal didn't care if anyone saw him. He scrambled to his feet, knocking out of the way the ancient swords and shields he'd been hiding behind on the balcony. Below him, men were surging towards the platform but he couldn't see what had caused the commotion.

What he *could* see was someone else on the balcony.

The archer smiled, hoisted a slim quiver of black feathered arrows onto his shoulder, and ducked quickly through an archway.

An archer? Who had he shot? There was a crumpled figure on the platform . . .

"No!" Mikal yelled, but his voice was lost in the noise of confusion. The image of Irvana's limp body burned into his vision.

Terenz and Davith reached Irvana at the same time; Terenz swept her into his arms and followed Davith, who was pushing the agitated Council members aside, clearing a path to the anteroom which Irvana had left only minutes ago.

It couldn't be happening.

"No one move! I will raise the alarm!" Davith shouted above the din. He sprinted the length of the chamber, his silver head disappearing under the balcony on which Mikal stood, unnoticed.

Mikal's insides twisted. The archer!

He snatched up an old-fashioned short sword and set off in pursuit of Irvana's attacker. He darted through the archway and took the stairs beyond two at a time. At the bottom he paused. Where was the man? Had he lost him? No, there he was, turning the corner at one end of the corridor. Mikal bolted after him, skidded round the same corner, and slid to a halt. The borrowed sword nearly slipped from his fingers.

Davith was about to drop a bag into the archer's outstretched hand.

The archer snatched his hand back, grabbed an arrow, and aimed the deadly barb of a black-feathered arrow at Mikal, pulling the string of the bow tight in readiness. "This one too, sir?"

Davith lunged at the archer and bright metal flashed.

The archer's arm jerked and he released the arrow, which brushed past Mikal's ear, soft as a breeze and sharp as a bee sting. A thin trickle of blood dribbled from the corner of the archer's mouth, then he slid to the floor making a horrible gurgling sound. Bubbles of blood burst on the archer's lips and spattered his chin until at last he fell silent, an expression of disbelief on his face.

"The danger is removed," Davith said.

Mikal's ear was still stinging. He touched the sore spot and looked at his fingers. They were red—the arrow must have nicked him. Unable to comprehend his narrow escape, Mikal forced himself to look away from the glassy eyes of the archer. Davith's face was twisted with an emotion he could not interpret. On the floor, at Davith's feet, lay the bag. Gold coins spilled from its mouth.

"You were giving him the money . . . you . . . ? To kill Irvana? But I thought you supported the StarMarks," Mikal whispered.

Davith slid a thin bladed knife back into a concealed sheath. "I do." Again, that strange expression played across his face.

"Then why?" Mikal almost wailed. "Why do this when you wanted the StarMark back?"

Davith took a step towards him.

"Oh no, you don't." Mikal thrust the sword out, standing

his ground. The point of the sword would not keep still, but it stopped Davith from advancing further.

"I have longed for the return of a golden Mark ever since Timat disappeared and threw Koltarn into turmoil." Davith's voice was quiet, but there was a hardness in his eyes, which made Mikal uneasy. "Why do you think I helped keep Terenz in power when others would have seen him deposed? I don't think even he realised what lengths I had to go to at times, to keep him where he was. For years I have supported him and removed opposition. No one can accuse me of being disloyal to the StarMarks."

"Irvana has a StarMark, too." Mikal tightened his grip on the sword.

Davith smiled. "It seems so simple, doesn't it? She does. But she's only a child. What does she know or understand about running a city?"

"She can learn. She has every right—"

"Every right?" Davith clenched his fist. "And what about Terenz? Do all his years of faithful service to Koltarn count for nothing? What about his rights?"

"I thought you liked Irvana." Mikal knew he was grasping at straws, trying to understand.

Davith inhaled sharply. "I do. But can you imagine how I felt when I realised that because of her, Terenz was likely to lose the overlordship? After all that I'd done to keep him there? I decided to do everything in my power to stop Timat's heir reaching Bernea, sent word of my intentions, but I failed in their execution. A good friend lost his life instead of Irvana."

An image of Niklos, lying bloodstained on the seat of a carriage, sprang into Mikal's head. "The bandits—that was you?"

"It's amazing what men will do for gold." Davith moved his hand slowly towards his sword. "But you had to play the hero. I had to rethink my plan." He sighed and his shoulders sagged a little. "Since we arrived here, I've spent time with Irvana.

She probably is Timat's daughter, you know. She has a certain way of holding her head, just like he used to. And she exhibits many of her mother's qualities. She *is* a lovely girl . . ." He ran a hand over his close-cropped head. "She confused me. I was torn between two StarMarks."

"And you picked Terenz," Mikal whispered.

Davith nodded. "For the good of Koltarn, you understand? A captain loyal to the overlords wouldn't prevent the coming of a golden Mark, he would embrace it. And I did. I chose the Black Star as having proved himself worthy of a golden Mark. I couldn't give it to a child, back from the dead, who had no understanding of the task ahead. With the StarChain returned to us and Irvana out of the way, Terenz can finally receive his due."

"It's not your decision to make. You won't succeed—I won't let you." Mikal almost choked on the words.

"You're too late, Mikal." Davith's handsome face twisted with contempt. "Irvana is already dead, by my order. What can you do now? Are you proposing to challenge me with that antique in your hand?" He smiled as he drew his own weapon. "Let's see what you can do then. Long live the Black Star!"

The clash of their swords echoed along the empty corridor. They struck blow after blow, Mikal fighting to hold his own against his more experienced opponent.

"Aaah!"

A burning slash of pain across his arm forced Mikal to break away. He willed himself not to faint. Davith had drawn first blood.

"Not bad," Davith panted, eyeing Mikal warily. "Your guardian has often told me he has little faith in your abilities, but I have to say you've surprised me. I am sorry it has to end this way though. How sad do you think Terenz will be, when I tell him that Irvana's assassin caught up with you as you fled the balcony, and I was too late to save your life before I killed him?"

"That's not going to happen." Mikal gritted his teeth and attacked, cutting and jabbing at Davith. He ignored his pain, allowing anger to drive his arm.

Taken by surprise, Davith was forced back a step. He stumbled over the foot of the dead archer behind him.

At the same time, Mikal thrust the sword out, felt it connect. He pulled it back quickly.

Davith dropped to his knees and slapped a hand to his ribs, his own sword falling to the ground with a clatter. He frowned at the blood oozing between his fingers. "Lucky strike. Long live the Black Star," he murmured and pitched face down onto the floor.

Davith was dead?

Mikal stared at Davith and flung his sword away. He retched, tasting bitterness and betrayal and guilt. He finally got control of his stomach and wiped his mouth on his sleeve. He had to get back, tell the Council what had happened, find out if . . .

Leaving behind the bloodied bodies, Mikal stumbled along the corridor on legs that would not stop trembling, injured arm held tight against his chest.

Some semblance of calm had been restored in the Council Chamber. None of the men took any notice of Mikal, even though he was dishevelled and bleeding. He kept to the edge of the silent crowd and headed towards the platform where their attention was focussed.

"—tragic that so shortly after she was found, my niece, Timat's daughter, has been taken from us." Terenz's voice broke. Murmurs of consolation filled the room.

So Irvana *was* dead. Davith had succeeded.

Mikal closed his eyes. When he opened them, he could barely see Terenz through his tears.

"She will not have died in vain," Terenz said. "We will honour Irvana for her role in returning the StarChain to us and in revealing the truth behind my brother's desertion of

Bernea, an event which has been a stain on his character for too long. Whilst I regret that we will never know the truth about her own claim, I will of course continue to uphold the duties of overlord, as I have always done—"

"A golden Mark! A gold star for Terenz!"

Many voices took up the solitary cry and Terenz held up a hand for silence, his grey eyes glittering. "If the Council deems it fitting, even in these unhappy circumstances, I would be honoured to wear the chain and finally validate my own claim to Koltarn."

Yells of support erupted from the chamber as Terenz turned towards Eran.

Eran, who had been standing silently beside Terenz, stirred as though waking from a deep sleep. Solemn faced, he held out the StarChain to Terenz.

Terenz took the chain and stared at it, weighing it in his hands, but made no move to put it on.

What was he waiting for? Mikal shifted uncomfortably as the tension mounted. Why was Terenz dragging the moment out?

Eran cleared his throat loudly. Terenz blinked and looked up. Eran nodded at the chain and raised his eyebrows.

Terenz passed the chain smoothly over his head and the diamond-studded star settled in the centre of his broad chest.

The whispers and furtive glances made Terenz's jaw tighten but he gave no other obvious sign that he was aware of anything wrong. Until the muttering grew louder. Then his composure snapped. He snatched the silver tray from the table, sending Timat's ring and the locket flying, and held the tray in front of his face. The seconds ticked by as he pulled at his skin, searching for the slightest glimmer of gold in his broken Mark. But the star on his cheek remained resolutely black.

Mikal sucked in a breath. A Mark only changed when the previous overlord was dead. Could it be—?

"She's alive!" someone shouted.

Terenz froze, still clutching the make-shift mirror.

"The arrow missed her heart," Faye called, pushing her way through the men towards the platform.

Lenad stepped out of the crowd to meet her. He caught his wife's hands and held them close to his chest. "She is gravely wounded?"

Faye nodded, on the verge of tears. "There is only a slim chance she will survive."

Lenad pulled her into an embrace.

Terenz flung the tray away from him with a shout.

"My Lord! Restrain yourself!" Eran thundered as it clattered down the steps. "This is good news. If Irvana survives—"

"Good?" Terenz snarled, whirling round on Eran, forcing him to take a step back. "If she survives, I will lose everything!"

"Which is why Davith arranged the assassination!" Mikal yelled.

"What nonsense is this?" Eran exclaimed. "Who speaks?"

Mikal stepped forward and the Council members craned their necks, jostling to see who had called out. He swallowed hard. He was going to have to stand against Terenz if Irvana was to be given any chance of success. "Davith wanted Terenz to have the golden Mark, not Irvana."

"And even if he did, am I to be held personally responsible for the misguided actions of every man who wishes to support me?" Terenz's eyes flashed with grey fire. "Let Captain Davith come forward and answer for himself."

"He can't . . . he's dead." Mikal had to raise his voice above the shouts of disbelief. "So is the assassin."

The Council dissolved into uproar. When order was eventually restored, Eran asked Mikal to recount all that he had seen and heard. Eran's brows knitted together when he heard how Mikal had sneaked onto the balcony, but he said nothing. Terenz remained stony-faced throughout the telling, even when Mikal repeated what Davith had implied—that the so-called Black Star had probably been aware of a plot to kill Irvana. By the time Mikal finished describing the fight for his life and the fatal wounding of Davith, the Council was deathly quiet.

"What is to be done in the face of these accusations?" Lenad demanded at last.

The Council fidgeted, looked at each other, at the banners, anywhere except at the platform where Terenz stood. No one said a word.

"Who do you believe—an overlord or an impertinent youth?" Terenz shouted at them. "I will swear, on my Mark, that I gave no direct order to Davith to remove Irvana. He acted alone and I am blameless in this matter." He took a deep breath and the golden disc glinted on his chest.

"But you tried to get rid of Irvana yourself, in Koltarn. I don't suppose that you tried very hard to stop him." Lenad's tone would have cut steel. "She told us what you did."

Terenz shrugged. "The child lied."

"No she didn'!" Rosann had come to stand beside Faye and Lenad now, her face tear-streaked but determined. "'E tried to choke 'er, back in Koltarn—I saw it all. That's 'ow 'is Mark got broken, I'll swear it to be true."

Mikal could have hugged Rosann.

"My Lord? Is that right?" Eran said.

Terenz lifted a hand towards his Mark. He stopped just short of touching it and hooked his hair behind his ear instead. His lip curled into a sneer. "There was an incident, yes."

He'd admitted it. Voices were again raised in disbelief and shock. Mikal stared, open-mouthed and silent, at Terenz.

"Did any of you think I would stand by and let a child take all this from me?" Terenz swept out his arm, encompassing not just the room, but all the trappings of power. "Any one of you would have done the same if you'd found yourself in my position." His eyes blazed. "The fact that I have a black star instead of a gold one has never affected my ability to be an effective member of this Council. If the girl had never appeared, you would all have been happy to allow that to continue. For thirteen years I have been—and I intend to remain—the overlord of Koltarn. Support me. You'll have to anyway, if the beet girl succumbs to her injury." His grey eyes surveyed the assembly, assessing, calculating.

"How can you ask us to support you, knowing that you tried to kill Irvana?" Lenad's voice shook with anger. "You have betrayed this Council, your own family, and everything that the StarMark stands for. You do not deserve to remain in the position."

The chamber filled with noise and confusion as every man tried to make his own view heard.

"Enough!" Eran roared. He waited for silence to fall. "From the moment Irvana's parentage was suspected, Lord Terenz's position in the line of succession was bound to be effected. Her lineage, if proven, would take precedence over his own. In that situation, I would have expected Lord Terenz to step aside as tradition demands. Instead, both he and certain of his supporters have taken steps to prevent this claim from succeeding, a thing inconceivable of anyone descended from the honourable StarMarks of Koltarn."

"Koltarn is mine. I will fight for it if I have to," Terenz said through gritted teeth.

"Can you not see the harm that will come if you persist with this folly?" Lenad shouted. "Give up your claim."

"Never."

Eran straightened his jacket, pushed his spectacles up his nose, and took a deep breath. "Koltarn's overlordship is contested and there is no verified claimant. In which case, it is written in the Council's statutes that the Prime Minister will temporarily fill the position until such time as a Mark can be verified. We shall give preference to and challenge the Mark of Irvana, Timat's daughter, when she recovers."

"If. Not when." Terenz shot a look of venomous hatred at Eran. He grabbed the StarChain which was still hanging around his neck and pulled. The chain snapped, and he threw the useless object at Eran's feet. "I need no golden star to prove my suitability. I have demonstrated my aptitude for the job of overlord to every single one of you." He pointed at the Council. "Who among the Council will support the Black Star for Koltarn?"

No one moved and Mikal hoped and prayed that no one would.

Then Robat stepped forward. "I offered my allegiance to Terenz as overlord of Koltarn when Timat abdicated his responsibilities. I see no reason to alter where my allegiance is placed." He jutted out his chin, as though daring any man to defy him.

Gant slid alongside Robat, his watchful eyes flicking from face to face. "I remain loyal to the Black Star."

Terenz stepped down from the platform and clasped Gant's hand, slapped Robat on the back. Together, the three of them strode towards the double doors, the rest of the Council parting before them like grass in the wind. A dozen or so moved to follow the Black Star. One of them had been standing close to Mikal.

"Please, give Irvana a chance." Mikal tried to pull the man back.

"Unhand me. My decision is made," the Councilman said.

Many more did not move. They simply watched.

At the door, Terenz turned to face those who had not joined him, his mouth set in a grim smile. "If the beet girl survives, she will find her support rather diminished and a fight on her hands. The Black Star *will* rule in Koltarn." He flung open the doors and marched out, his supporters jostling each other as they followed.

CHAPTER 21
Gold, at Last

IRVANA DRIFTED IN and out of the deep blackness, a constant ache in her chest. Snatches of conversation reached her through a pain-filled haze.

" . . . you must watch for signs of infection . . ."

" . . . no improvement, Mikal . . ."

" . . . don' you give up, Irvana, keep fightin' . . ."

" . . . couldn't bear it, not after Katrin . . ."

None of it made any sense, until the day she remembered the black-feathered arrow and opened her eyes long enough to see Faye sitting beside the bed.

"Why are you crying?" she whispered. "I'm not dead."

But it took a long while before she felt fully alive again. Her body worked hard to repair the arrow's damage, but the slightest effort left her weak and exhausted.

The leaves on the trees had begun to change from summer green to autumn hues before Irvana was strong enough to get out of bed and lay on a couch by the window with Lenad's old boarhound guarding her, listening to Mikal reading aloud or watching Faye's needle flash in and out of her embroidery.

No one ever talked about the presentation and what had happened. And did she really want to know, Irvana wondered. Someone had tried hard to make sure she was not the next overlord of Koltarn, that much she knew . . . but who? Terenz? She hadn't seen Davith since the attack—perhaps he was dealing with an investigation? And what about Terenz? How had he reacted? When she couldn't bear not knowing any longer, she asked—and Lenad told her.

She'd thought that nothing could be worse than having

an arrowhead dug out of her chest, but betrayal hurt even
more. Davith? Davith had wanted her dead? She bent double
and pressed a hand to her chest. Was the pain she felt there
the arrow wound, irritated by her gasping sobs, or her heart,
breaking?

By the time she'd calmed down, Lenad had told her all
about Terenz too.

"He still won't give up the overlordship?" Irvana didn't
know how much more bad news she could take. Was there
any good in all of this?

"He calls 'imself the Black Star all the time now, an' them
who are daft enough to support 'im are running round, trying
to persuade anyone who'll listen to let 'im keep the job,"
Rosann chipped in.

"Surely, Eran's going to do something about it?"

Lenad huffed and tugged his beard. "Yes. He's going
to challenge your Mark and settle the issue of Koltarn's
overlord—one way or another."

It wasn't worth holding the second presentation in the
Council Chamber. For a start, there were only a few Council
members who remained undecided or who wholeheartedly
supported Irvana's claim—they would barely fill the platform,
let alone the entire chamber. And Irvana wasn't really strong
enough yet to stand for long—least of all in the place where a
single arrow had caused so much hurt.

Instead, everyone squeezed their way into Lenad's
apartments; Eran, Faye, Lenad, Rosann, Mikal, and a handful
of Councilmen. Every eye was fixed on Irvana, seated in
Lenad's chair by the fireplace.

She wore the ruby red silk dress today—it was her
favourite, and if it was to be the last time she wore it . . . She
twirled the end of one of her plaits as she waited—Faye had
plaited Irvana's hair on either side so that the StarMark was
visible. There would be no hiding it today.

"I will not stand on ceremony," Eran said, pushing his

spectacles up his nose. "We all know why we are here. Irvana, are you ready?"

Was she? Irvana went hot, then cold. She had no choice—she had to know, one way or the other. She pushed herself to her feet on legs that trembled. "I'm ready."

Eran stepped towards her with the StarChain in his hands, the diamonds sparkling almost as much as the new chain.

Irvana carefully took it from him and felt the same tingle in her fingers that she had when she'd first held it. Quickly, she slipped the chain over her head and turned away from everyone.

She waited, though she wasn't sure what for. Then—

"Ow!" The nape of her neck was burning!

"It's turning. Good gods, it's actually turning!" she heard one of the Councilmen mutter.

She resisted the urge to slap a hand to her neck and gritted her teeth against the pain. The heat faded quickly, leaving her skin tingling. Irvana turned back to face the assembled witnesses. Faye had tears in her eyes, Rosann was doing a strange little dance, and Lenad was pumping Mikal's hand up and down. Even the Councilmen looked pleased.

Eran beamed. "I think we can say your claim is very much verified, Irvana. Congratulations!"

"It's gold?" she whispered. "I am really Timat's daughter?"

"Very much so." Eran clapped his hands. "Time for a celebration."

The door opened and servants entered, carrying trays of food and drink.

Irvana sank into the chair again and in a daze, received the congratulations that were offered from the depleted Council.

"It's a beautiful Mark," Rosann told her.

"Is it?" Irvana rubbed the back of her neck. "I wish I could see it."

Rosann frowned, then her face lit up. "I've got an idea. Come wi'me!" She took Irvana's hand and led her into the bedroom. "Now, you sit there." She pointed to the stool in front of the dressing table. "Let me get this in the right place, and—" She angled a hand mirror until the back of Irvana's neck was reflected in the larger one.

"Oh!"

There it was—a golden star, gleaming on the nape of her neck. Proof—that she was an overlord's daughter. Irvana beamed at Rosann. No wonder everyone was smiling.

The only person who seemed unhappy about how things had turned out was Mikal.

"Eran should've done more, made this presentation a huge event. The Black Star wouldn't have settled for a quick hand over." He bit angrily into a slice of cake.

"Don't call him that," Irvana said.

"Sorry."

Irvana fingered the spot on her neck where she knew there was now a shining star. It was still tingling slightly. Its golden presence confirmed that she was truly a member of the StarMark dynasty, but it looked as though she was going to have to fight to be recognised as the overlord of Koltarn. She didn't know whether to feel relieved or dismayed.

"I'm not Terenz and I'm perfectly happy with what's happened." That was certainly true—she'd dreaded the prospect of standing in the Council Chamber again.

Mikal's lips twitched.

Irvana nudged him. "What?"

With the cake still in his hand, he performed an elaborate bow, showering her with crumbs. "Little orphan Irvana, now a great overlord." He straightened up. "I wonder what your first order will be. For the good folk of Koltarn to offer their allegiance to their new overlord? Or maybe . . . maybe it will be to demand that all future bearers of the Mark must spend several weeks peeling potatoes in the palace kitchen before claiming their birthright?"

"Of course not." Was that a joke? Irvana couldn't be sure.

Mikal was in such an odd mood today—she'd thought he would be pleased that her Mark was real, but it didn't seem to be the case. Well, she'd make sure she had the last laugh. "I think my first order will be . . ." She narrowed her eyes in imitation of Terenz, and was delighted to see Mikal look decidedly worried. "To order dinner. With Black Beetroot pudding for dessert."

"Why, you—" Mikal thumped her.

"Ow! Don't you know you're not supposed to hit overlords?" Irvana regretted it as soon as she said it.

A shutter came down over Mikal's face. "Eran wants you. My lady." He turned away.

"It was a joke!"

Mikal ignored her and helped himself to more food.

"Be like that then." Irvana sighed and reluctantly joined Eran, who was standing with Lenad.

"We must act, and act quickly," Lenad was saying, underlining his words by thumping his fist into the palm of his hand.

"I agree. He must be stopped." Eran pinched the bridge of his nose.

He'd changed since the first presentation. His eyes were deeply shadowed and the elegant jackets which used to strain at the seams now hung loose on his frame. He replaced his spectacles with a sigh.

"We have the law on our side and could arrest Terenz. It is written in the constitution of Koltarn that anyone who threatens an overlord shall be detained for treason, even if they themselves are in the line of succession. But we do not have sufficient manpower to defeat him, especially if our sources are to be believed. He has commandeered the support of the majority of the other overlords. They *will* fight." He rubbed at the frown lines etched deeply into his forehead.

Lenad nodded but leaned closer, speaking urgently. "You've said yourself that Terenz will probably not consider open war before the spring, because he's still hoping for a bloodless coup with the majority behind him. But we could arrest him before then. I've been tracking his movements for some time. He's using Robat's forest lodge as a base, travels with just a few soldiers for speed. Right now, he's visiting Jeram, hoping to persuade him to switch sides before snow prevents further travel. You know the weather's already closing in—the first flurries of snow fell here yesterday. If we move fast, we could intercept Terenz before he digs in at Robat's for the winter. What do you say? If we remove him then any resistance will hopefully wither away. We'll be able to instate Irvana as planned in Koltarn."

Eran held up his hands. "It is not that simple, Lenad. Remember that we now have an overlord of Koltarn who must be consulted. We cannot decide for her. Irvana?"

Uh-oh. Irvana squirmed. What did she know about politics or power struggles? She'd only just got the golden star, wasn't ready for this. She'd much rather forget about Terenz . . . get on with her own life and leave him to his.

Of course, that was impossible. Terenz wouldn't stop now. Not until he'd got rid of her and regained the position he seemed to think she'd stolen from him.

What would her father have done? Irvana had been finding out more and more about Timat. By all accounts he had been firm yet fair. Everyone she had spoken to held him in high regard, because in his brief time as overlord, he had always done everything in his power to maintain peace in his city.

Perhaps her first real decision as overlord must be one that achieved the same goal.

"Terenz is family. He's my uncle and he has a Mark," she said. "But I'm the one with a golden star. I know I have to think of the people of Koltarn now, but I can't ignore everyone else. Terenz is stirring up all the overlords, might drag them into a fight that will affect thousands. If he has to be arrested to stop that, then that's what we'll do."

Irvana felt her cheeks grow warm as polite applause broke

out. She hadn't realised everyone had been listening to her. They wouldn't be applauding by the time she'd finished. "Terenz knows a lot about the overlordship, and it would be silly to lose that. His arrest will mean there's no war, but I don't want him to be jailed. I want him to help me."

"Really? In spite of everything he's done? Do you understand what you're saying?" Eran's eyes were wide behind his spectacles.

Irvana nodded. "He's the only family I've got. And he should be recognised for what he's done for Koltarn. The city obviously means a lot to him, he only wants what's best for it." Out of the corner of her eye, she saw Mikal watching her.

"Irvana, are you sure?" Lenad asked.

"I'm sure." Terenz might not agree, of course, but Irvana had to give him that chance.

Eran wasted no time. A scribe was summoned, who drew up the arrest warrant immediately. Irvana signed her name on the parchment—her shaky signature, written next to a tiny drawing of her coat of arms, was proof of her decision. Eran blotted the ink dry, sealed the parchment with wax, and stamped it with his own ring. The Council, such as it was, was dismissed.

Irvana sank into a chair as Eran made to leave. He paused on the threshold.

"With great power comes great responsibility, Irvana. You are still young to bear so much. The decisions that need to be made as overlord are not always easy, but you must try not to make them harder for yourself. I hope you know what you're doing, asking Terenz to advise you."

"So do I," she murmured as Eran left.

CHAPTER 22
A Fatal Encounter

A FEW DAYS later, Irvana stared out at the pine forest surrounding Bernea while the trees of another forest, miles away, swayed in the wind.

A light shower of leaves rained down on Mikal and he brushed them off. How much longer did they have to wait?

"Someone's coming."

The whispered warning ran down the line of concealed men until it reached Lenad who was standing with the tethered horses. His grip tightened on the warrant he was holding.

"Is it him?" Mikal shivered.

"We must wait for confirmation." Lenad stroked the nose of his horse. "There's no need to be scared. You'll be safe if you stay here."

"I'm just cold." This far south, there was no sign of snow yet, but the late autumn air was chilly and damp. That's why Mikal was shivering. He wasn't scared. But as the moment of confrontation drew closer, he wasn't so sure that was true.

"There's the signal."

A flash of blue came from the depths of a bush on the opposite side of the gorge. Their quarry had been sighted.

"I must go." Lenad started to walk away.

Mikal followed.

Lenad whirled round. "I told you, Mikal, you have to stay here. It'll be far too dangerous. Don't leave the horses." He headed down the path again.

Mikal sighed, but stayed put. It wasn't fair. He wanted to see what happened, deserved to. Terenz *had* been his guardian. Instead, all he got to do was look after the horses, and the animals obviously didn't need him.

What if he went just a bit further down the path . . . ?

Lenad would be disappointed in him, a voice inside Mikal's head said.

I just want to get a bit closer, he argued with himself. *To find somewhere I can see without being seen. Where's the harm in that? Lenad will never know . . .*

Mikal crept down the path towards a large rhododendron bush. He wormed his way into its middle and peered through the gaps in the leaves.

The path continued to slope down until it met a narrow wood-and-rope bridge stretched across a ravine. The river at the bottom of the gorge ran swift and deep. Lenad had called the site a perfect trap.

Mikal heard the sound of hooves and a horse burst into view from the trees on the opposite side of the gorge.

The black stallion pulled up sharply and pawed at the ground, his flanks heaving and sweating, his black-clothed rider sitting comfortably in the saddle. Even from this distance, Mikal had no difficulty in recognising Terenz.

Mikal shivered again. This time it was most definitely not because he was cold.

Terenz's dark hair was windswept from the ride. He flicked it out of his eyes as half-a-dozen mounted soldiers caught up with him at the bridge.

"Look on the bright side." Robat's voice carried clearly to Mikal's hiding place. "Jeram refuses to be persuaded, but you still have many others who will stand behind you."

"How can he so easily dismiss all that I've given to Koltarn?" Terenz replied.

Mikal recognised that tone of voice. Terenz's brows would be knitted together in a scowl.

"How can he possibly continue to support the beet girl? She may well have a golden Mark now, but by all accounts it is Eran who handles the city's business. The girl is a mere puppet. Gah!" Terenz persuaded his stallion onto the swaying bridge, followed by a couple of the soldiers and their mounts.

"'Tis glad I am, that this is our last trip before the winter truly catches up with us," Robat called as he waited for his turn to cross. "I must be getting old. My bones never used to feel the cold like this. I remember campaigns where we slept in the snow and thought only that it would toughen us up. Now, I long for the fire and a warm bed." He roared with laughter and several of the soldiers laughed with him.

Terenz urged his horse about two thirds of the way over the gorge and then stopped. Why? Mikal shifted position until he saw the lone figure blocking the exit from the bridge: Lenad.

"Make way. Allow me off the bridge," Terenz shouted, his voice echoing off the walls of the ravine.

"That, I cannot agree to," Lenad called back. "I have a warrant for your arrest, filing charges of treason against the StarMark of Koltarn."

"What?" Terenz snorted. "You appear very confident, Lenad. You are one, and we are many. Do you think you will succeed, considering the odds?"

"I think we can move things a little in my favour." Lenad raised his hand.

At his signal, there was a rustling from the undergrowth and twenty or more archers emerged from their hiding places on both sides of the canyon. Every man's arrow was notched firmly in place, pointing at the men still waiting to cross and at Terenz, now trapped on the bridge. Robat cursed loudly.

"I suggest that in the face of such overwhelming odds," Lenad shouted, "you advise your men to drop their weapons and surrender. You will be treated as prisoners of state until such time as we return to Bernea."

With a sound like a sigh, Terenz's sword slid smoothly out of its scabbard, the blade flashing silver against his dark jacket. "My men may surrender if they wish, but I have no intention of giving up so easily. For the Black Star!" Brandishing the weapon above his head, Terenz spurred his horse onwards, ignoring the shouts of his men and the bridge swinging wildly under him. He reached solid ground and kicked his horse towards Lenad.

They were going to fight—his guardian and his master! Mikal fought his way out of the bush, scratching face and arms in his haste. He scrambled and slid down the path towards the nearest archer.

"What are you waiting for?" he yelled. "Fire!"

"They're too close together. Keep back, boy, out of the way." The soldier shoved Mikal away from him.

Lenad and Terenz were fighting near the edge of the ravine. The Black Star had the advantage of being on horseback and Lenad was being hard pressed. A blow sent Lenad sprawling. Terenz leapt from the saddle and advanced towards him.

"He'll kill him!" Mikal yelled. He bolted down the path and threw himself onto Terenz's back, clinging tight, hammering at Terenz's unprotected head. "Stop it! Stop!"

Terenz gave a mighty heave of his broad shoulders and flung Mikal off sideways. He landed with a thud.

"Ooof!"

Terenz snarled and spun round. His eyes flashed with recognition when he looked down. "Mikal?"

"You don't have to do this," Mikal gasped. "Irvana wants your help, you can still be involved in Koltarn. You—"

An arrow thudded into Terenz's shoulder. He yelled and stumbled, dangerously close to the edge of the gorge.

Lenad struggled to his feet and staggered forward, sword slashing wildly. Terenz caught sight of him and tried to twist away, but Lenad's blade snagged in the black jacket.

Terenz's stallion gave a scream of pain and reared up, an arrow buried deep in its flank.

Terenz cowered beneath flailing hooves, which crashed to the ground a hands-breadth away from him. The stallion reared up a second time, its eyes rolling madly. The deadly hooves descended again, caught Terenz a glancing blow, and knocked him off balance.

With a cry, he fell into the ravine.

"No!" Mikal crawled to the edge of the gorge and stared down into the waters below. Where was he? There—a hand—reaching out of the water, a flash of silver visible before it was sucked back under. A dark shape was tossed and whirled about, carried away in the speeding river.

"We have to help him!" Mikal leaned out as far as he dared, trying not to lose sight of Terenz. He tipped forward, stones and earth tumbling down as the cliff crumbled beneath him. A fierce tug on his jacket jerked him back onto solid ground. Mikal scrambled to his feet, ready to run, but someone kept hold of his arm.

"We can't help," Lenad snapped. "No one can get down there fast enough. We'll look for him further downstream."

Mikal pointed at a black speck in the water, almost out of sight. "The rapids! He'll be bashed to pieces against the rocks." Feeling sick, he tore his arm free.

"I know. I didn't wish that for him," Lenad muttered, his face drawn. He grabbed Mikal's arm again and shook him violently. "What were you thinking, jumping on Terenz like that? He could have killed you. You were unarmed and disobeyed a direct order. How stupid can you get?"

"I thought I could stop you from killing him." Mortified to find that his eyes were prickling with tears, Mikal fought Lenad off. "He looked after me."

Lenad's face crumpled and he seized Mikal into a crushing hug. Then he held him at arm's length, his own eyes glistening. "I understand. It was a brave, foolish thing you did, but it saved my life. We'll save Terenz, too—he's tough, won't be hurt badly."

Really? Mikal didn't think so. But they had to try to rescue the Black Star—for Irvana . . .

"Sergeant, get the rest of this motley crew rounded up," Lenad called. "Perhaps the loss of their leader will cool their enthusiasm for a fight. We're going fishing."

The prisoners were sent back to Bernea under heavy guard. Only Lenad, Mikal, and a handful of archers followed the route of the winding gorge, searching in its depths for any sign of Terenz. The roar of water was deafeningly loud as, far below them, the river thundered over jumbled rocks, sending a mist of spray high into the air.

They searched until the light faded, plunging the bottom of the gorge into even deeper gloom.

"Can't see a thing now. We'll continue tomorrow," Lenad said.

"Do you think we'll find him?" Mikal was annoyed to hear a tremor in his voice.

Lenad shrugged. "Perhaps . . . But if I'm honest, I'm starting to think it unlikely. The rapids are fuller than I've ever seen them."

A shudder took hold of Mikal. The water was so deep, so fast, it would have been able to carry a body easily, dashing it against the jagged rocks repeatedly with such force . . . "What do we tell Irvana?"

Lenad sighed and tugged his beard. "That The Black Star is dead. That she has the golden star and no one stands between her and her inheritance, but she's going to have to manage it alone."

CHAPTER 23
The Great Fair

AS THE CONVOY of carriages emerged from the forest, Irvana shaded her eyes against the brightness of the summer sun. The view was exactly as she remembered it. Nothing had changed—except her.

A year ago, when she had reached this point in the road, she'd been wearing patched clothes and had sat squashed between baskets of fruit and vegetables on the back of a rattling cart.

Now, she was dressed in silk and travelling in comfort on velvet cushions in an open-topped carriage. She was followed by Faye and Rosann and an entourage of servants. *And* she was overlord of the city which lay at the end of the road. Over her head fluttered a blue banner and she felt a surge of pride for the gold star nestling in its cream shell.

Lenad rode up beside the carriage. "How does it feel to be back?"

"Strange."

Mikal rode up on her other side. "You'll get used to it."

"When we get into the city itself, expect it to be busy," Lenad said. "We'll go straight to the palace, avoid the crowds."

"Isn't it always busy?" Irvana asked.

Mikal rolled his eyes and tutted. "It's the first day of the fair."

"Is it? Can we go? Please, Lenad? I only saw the hiring stand last year." Irvana leaned out of the carriage in her eagerness.

"Not a good idea," Lenad said. "Maybe tomorrow, once we've unpacked."

Irvana dropped back into her seat, disappointed. She really,

really wanted to wander through the fair, see everything she'd missed twelve months ago. She ought to be able to do what she liked. A plan took shape in her mind. She grinned and sat up straighter. "Lenad . . . as overlord of Koltarn, I can do as I please in my city, can't I?"

Lenad frowned. "Ye-ess, you can, but if you would take my advice—"

"Then I'm going to the fair. Today."

The argument lasted almost to the city gates, but nothing Lenad said would make Irvana change her mind. She didn't care about the unpacking, didn't think anyone would mind if she turned up at the palace later than expected, and she also reminded Lenad that as he'd sworn allegiance to her, he couldn't say no.

"Very well," he growled. "If you are determined, then we will proceed only if you agree to stay by my side at all times."

"I promise." She'd won. Irvana wriggled on her cushion, trying not to look too pleased with herself.

"We will not draw attention to ourselves," Lenad said. "The servants will go on to the palace as originally planned. You and I will spend only a short time in the market before we follow them. Agreed?"

Mikal frowned. "What about me? Am I being lumped in with the servants?"

"Well, you are Lenad's page, so I suppose . . . yes," Irvana said. "It's just me and Lenad going to the fair."

"Thank you for pointing that out," Mikal snarled back. "At least I know exactly where I stand." He let his horse drop back.

"Irvana, that was unkind," Lenad said, quietly.

"But it's true. I can't help it if he takes it the wrong way."

"I can always change my mind if you don't behave, even if you are the overlord."

Irvana fell silent. She didn't want to give Lenad any excuse to take her straight home. Home . . . the palace was going to be her home. As her excitement mounted, she put Mikal to the back of her mind and focussed on the city.

Once they were safely inside the city wall, Irvana swapped her carriage for one of the servants' horses. She grinned at Mikal as he rode past following the coaches heading up the hill. He didn't even look at her. Irvana shrugged. Not her fault if he was grumpy.

No one knew her here, yet. Oh, they knew of the change in overlordship, but no one knew her face. And she was thankful of that as she followed Lenad through the narrowing streets towards the great market. There would be plenty of time for recognition later in the month, when Eran came to formally introduce her to the citizens of Koltarn. For now, she would travel unnoticed, pretending to be an ordinary girl travelling with a favourite uncle.

She giggled at the thought.

Lenad twisted in his saddle to look at her. "What's so funny?"

"It's nothing, I'm just happy to be back," she said, fighting back a grin.

They dismounted at the edge of the market square and Lenad threw a silver coin towards a young boy. "Watch our horses while we attend to business and there'll be another of those when we return."

The lad grinned and pocketed his good fortune. "I'll look after 'em good, sir, you'll see. I'll water 'em and groom 'em too, if you like?"

"Very well. Mind you don't skimp on the grooming."

There was so much to see. Irvana darted between the stalls, Lenad doing his best to keep up with her. She sampled hard cheese, cut into wedges and edged with black wax rind; buried her fingers in the thick fleeces of spotted sheep; sniffed at spices and herbs in their baskets, sneezing when she got too close to the pepper. And the scarves! They fluttered and waved in the breeze, as soft as cobwebs to the touch.

Irvana ran one through her fingers. "Aren't they beautiful?" For some reason, she thought of Aymee. The old lady might not be able to see the colours, but she would love the feel of them. "Lenad . . . I'd like to buy some presents. But . . ."

Lenad chuckled. "And I thought it was just Faye who could make my coins disappear. Here." He handed Irvana a purse. "Buy what you want and we'll settle the accounting when Eran arrives later in the week."

"Thank you."

Irvana went from stall to stall. She found a bright yellow scarf for Aymee, a decorated mirror for Rosann, skeins of coloured embroidery thread for Faye, and a pair of handsome leather riding gloves for Mikal.

"It's getting late. We've spent far too long here already. We really must be going," Lenad said.

"Oh, but I haven't got everything yet," Irvana protested.

"We'll come back tomorrow. Bring Mikal and Rosann with us. Won't that be more fun?" Lenad was already hurrying her back to the horses.

"I suppose so, but—"

As they passed the hiring stand, Irvana saw that it was as full as when she had stood inside it. Even today, there was a young girl, wearing a faded dress and a tentative smile, standing alone and a little apart from the others. She had a bag at her feet, just like that other girl from what seemed like a lifetime ago.

Irvana stopped walking. What would this other girl's future be? She certainly wouldn't end up as an overlord, would she? But what could she be doing instead? "Lenad, wait."

"Irvana, we must be getting back. I told you, there's no more time for shopping—"

"Please. I want you to do something for me."

Lenad sighed. "What?"

"See that girl?" Irvana pointed her out. "Will you ask her to come up to the palace tomorrow, report to the kitchen? I'm sure Merty could always use an extra pair of hands."

Lenad's eyes crinkled as he smiled. "I think we can take a few minutes more. I'll ask her."

Irvana watched as he approached the girl, chewing at a thumbnail until the girl's worried expression melted away and broke into an incredulous smile. When Lenad came back, Irvana grabbed his arm. "Well? Is she going to come?"

"She'll report to the palace kitchen tomorrow, as you requested."

"Good. Now we can go." Irvana felt a warm glow in her chest. Was this what it felt like, to be able to help her people? Her people . . . There and then, she vowed always to help the people of Koltarn. She would feed those who were hungry, buy shoes for the street urchins who ran barefoot, make sure that no one had to sell their children ever again . . . then she remembered. Lenad's present. She frowned. They'd walked right past the stall selling pipes and tobacco and were back where they'd left their mounts.

The young groom was waiting for them with the horses. "'Ere you go, sir. Fresh as daisies."

Lenad gave the horses a quick inspection. "You've done a good job. Here, catch." He tossed a coin at the boy, who snatched it out of the air.

"Any time, sir, any time." With a grin, he ran off and was soon lost in the crowd.

Lenad offered his cupped hands to help Irvana mount, but she hesitated.

"What is it now?" he said. "More strays to help?"

"No." Irvana bit her lip. "I really need to buy one more thing, or someone will be left out. I'll go on my own. The stall's not far away, and I'll come straight back."

Lenad shook his head. "Not on your own. I'll find someone to hold the horses again."

"But that will spoil the surprise."

"I'm not going to tell—" Lenad stopped mid-sentence and gave his beard a tug. "Ah . . . I see . . . Something for me?"

Irvana nodded.

"The stall's not far away you say? Hmm . . . Be as quick as you can and come straight back here. I'll be waiting."

"Thank you." Irvana stood on tiptoe and placed a light kiss on his cheek before skipping away. She glanced over her shoulder, but the crowds had already closed in. Lenad couldn't see her now.

For the first time in months, she was truly on her own. Freedom!

The tobacco stall was further into the market than she remembered—she thought maybe she'd missed it. But then she smelt pipe smoke and followed her nose to the table filled with baskets of dried tobacco leaves. She breathed in their scent, trying to decide whether Lenad would prefer the richness of apple and cinnamon tobacco or the tangier orange one.

"Apple and cinnamon, please. How much will this buy me?" Irvana held a silver coin out to the stall holder.

"Almost a year's supply," the man said, talking round the pipe still clamped firmly in his teeth. "Tell you what. Why don't I chop up a good handful of leaves and then we'll stick 'em in one of these luvly leather pouches I've got? Make it a bit more like a present, as I'm guessing it ain't goin' to be you that smokes the stuff?"

Irvana thought for a moment. Lenad already had a tobacco pouch, but it was old and worn. The stall holder's suggestion would make a far better present. "Alright. Thank you."

Her purchase made, she wandered slowly back to Lenad, making the most of her time alone. A face in the crowd made her pause. "Matild!"

The woman looked to see who'd called and frowned. Irvana thought she must have been mistaken, but then the woman's face broke into a wide smile. "Irvana, is that you?"

Matild and Irvana moved quickly towards each other, just as an old man stepped into Matild's path. They collided, the man knocked off balance by the impact.

"Oh, sir, I'm so sorry!" Matild steadied him. "There you go, you're still on your feet. Alright now? Good. Now, where was—"

She looked up, spotted Irvana, and reached her without further incident.

"Look at you!" Matild crushed Irvana in a warm embrace and then held her arm's length. "So tall . . . and happy. And what a lovely dress. Silk? My, oh my." She pulled Irvana towards a row of carts. "Come, Simean will be so glad to see you. He oft remarked after last summer that he hoped you'd found the man you needed. I think he was worried, the big soft-hearted fellow. There he is, look."

Simean was standing beside the same plain cart. He was red faced and held a screaming baby in each arm. He spotted Matild.

"What kept you? They're hungry, woman!" he bellowed above the din.

Matild whipped a baby from him and settled herself on the back board of the cart. Within seconds the baby had stopped screaming and Simean passed the second baby to Matild.

Irvana took her fingers out of her ears, relieved that the bawling had stopped.

Simean turned towards her and did a double-take. "Why, if it isn't the fairy child we found in the forest." He picked Irvana up and swung her round a couple of times. "'Tis glad I am to see you. And looking so well." He set her back on solid ground.

"You're a father?" Irvana laughed, feeling breathless and giddy.

"Aye. Don't know quite how that happened—"

"In the usual way," Matild interrupted with a laugh.

Simean grinned sheepishly. "Two lusty boys, Aran and Peyter, and they're the apples of their papa's eye." He turned to serve a customer.

"There you are!"

Irvana had forgotten all about Lenad.

He strode towards her, red-faced and beard bristling, one hand on his sword. "Do you know how long you have been gone?"

"Oh . . . er . . ." Irvana quickly shoved the tobacco up her sleeve. "I'm sorry. I saw Matild . . . I told you about her and Simean. They helped me last summer. Remember?"

"I see." Lenad's colour faded. "Then I am pleased to meet you." He bowed.

"This was the man you were looking for?" Matild said, eyeing Lenad approvingly over the heads of her babies.

"Oh no," Irvana said. "That was Matteuw, but he wouldn't help me. Lenad's my escort."

Matild gasped. "What? But he's old enough to be your grandfather."

"He's not that old."

"Irvana, when a gentleman is escorting a lady," Lenad spluttered, "it usually means that there is an agreement of marriage between them."

Irvana could feel the heat rising in her cheeks. "That's not—no. I mean, you're looking after me, but not like—"

A strange cry interrupted her. She looked at where Simean had been serving. The customer, a man, lay on the ground, his limbs twitching uncontrollably.

"What's happened? What's wrong with him?" Irvana gripped Lenad's arm. Had the man been attacked in broad daylight?

"'Tis only Rojer. Don't mind him, dearie," a nearby woman said. "He 'as these turns. 'E'll be right as rain in no time."

"Are you sure? Can't we do anything?" Irvana had made a vow to help her people and here was another who needed her assistance.

"No, not without drawing attention to ourselves," Lenad hissed, taking Irvana's arm firmly. "It's getting late and we should be going. Others will come to his aid."

"I'm not going to leave without doing something." She pulled a gold coin from Lenad's purse.

"Am I going to have any money left?" Lenad grumbled.

Irvana ignored him. "Matild, will you give him this? Tell him it's for a doctor."

Matild's eyes widened at the sight of gold. "Irvana, where did you . . . Gold?"

"Shh!" Irvana glanced round, suddenly fearful. "Just do it, please."

Matild stared at her over the heads of the babies. "What's going on, Irvana?"

Before she could answer, Lenad grabbed her arm. "We really must leave. People are looking."

"Wait!" Irvana shook him off, grabbed Matild's hand, and pressed the coin into it. "Come to the palace, tomorrow. You and Simean and the babies. I'll explain everything then, honest."

"But—"

"Tomorrow," she said.

Lenad took hold of Irvana's arm again.

"Tomorrow," Irvana repeated, and allowed Lenad to steer her away.

CHAPTER 24
Memories

ROJER CAME TO his senses, groaned, and then cursed. Damn these fits!

There was no shortage of hands ready to help him up, but he shook them off impatiently and limped away from the scene of his embarrassment.

"Here, you forgot your apples," a woman called. "And the young lady left you a coin for a physician."

Pain sliced through his head. He groaned and clutched at the broad streak of long white hair which covered half his scalp and hung over his face.

Someone grabbed his arm and he pushed it away. "Leave me be. I need no doctor."

"Are you certain? You don't look—"

Rojer lifted his head.

The man who'd sold him the apples recoiled.

"I don't look what?" He waited, but the apple seller didn't answer. The sight of Rojer's face usually struck folk dumb.

"Gah!" He stumbled away, dragging his crippled leg.

Rojer limped straight into the nearest tavern, stopping several times on the way. Each time he stopped, he gritted his teeth and grasped his head with shaking hands while he waited for the pain to pass.

Inside the busy alehouse, Rojer threw a couple of coppers onto the bar. "Beer."

He took the full tankard and dropped heavily onto a free bench, then drained half the beer in greedy gulps. His thirst quenched, he banged the tankard onto the bench so hard, some of the remaining beer spilled over the top. He began to draw patterns in the liquid.

Rojer stopped drawing, his finger finishing on the tip of a seven-pointed star. He stared at what he'd drawn, then got unsteadily to his feet, knocking the tankard to the floor. It rolled under the bench but he ignored it. Wild-eyed, he pushed his way out of the crowded inn.

He stumped through the market, forcing a path through the crowds, searching for one face in particular. Eventually, he saw it.

His . . . sister . . . was absorbed in conversation. Neither she nor her gentleman friend noticed him. He stopped an arm's length away to listen.

" . . . why can't we act? He seems so much better." His sister wrung her hands.

"He isn't!" her companion snapped. "He's never going to be able to go back, not now. This idea of yours is nothing but madness!"

His sister winced.

The gentleman twirled his ridiculous moustache. "My dear, you must realise that there is no hope. Things will never be the same as they were. He has no memory of any of it."

"But I could explain? Perhaps that would help. I'm sure—" She glanced sideways, spotting Rojer. "You're back! I was wondering where you'd got to. Did you remember the apples?"

"Apples?"

"Oh, Rojer." She pressed a hand to her chest, where she wore the ring on the chain.

"And you tell me he is improving? You are wasting your time, my dear. Best to let sleeping dogs lie. Good day to you." A swift kiss on the lady's hand, a nod of the head, and the gentleman was gone.

"Never mind." She took Rojer's hand. "Let's go back. I'll help you remember—"

"I don't need any help to remember." His grip tightened on her hand, making her flinch.

"Rojer! You're hurting me!"

He stared deep into her green eyes. Pain stabbed through his head again and he gritted his teeth against it.

"My name is not Rojer," he growled.

CHAPTER 25
Cracks

IRVANA RODE UP to the front door of the palace. Mikal was standing on the steps, hands on his hips, a frown on his face. "About time. We've been waiting for ages for the overlord of Koltarn to show her face."

Irvana dismounted, excited. "I couldn't help it. I met someone in the market, stopped to talk—"

Mikal ignored her. He grabbed the reins and led her horse away, his body stiff with anger.

Irvana stared after him. Why was he so mad with her? She knew he hadn't liked being sent on with the servants, but he didn't usually hold a grudge or take it so much to heart.

"Don't mind him. Come and greet the staff," Lenad said. "They've been waiting too."

How could she not have noticed the double line of navy-clad servants standing either side of the door at the top of the steps? Irvana swallowed hard. What would they say when they recognised the girl who used to peel potatoes, the girl who had left them thinking she was a thief?

On shaking legs, she began to climb towards them. What would Merty say? Would she tell Irvana to stop pretending to be something she wasn't and get back to work in the kitchens?

No. Merty simply bobbed a curtsey as Irvana drew level. "My lady, welcome. It's good to have you back with us."

"Really? You knew it was me?" Irvana blinked at her. "Does that mean you know—"

Merty nodded. "The Prime Minister was good enough to send a letter, informing us of your arrival and explaining everything." She leaned closer. "There will be no references to the time before, when, you know . . ."

Irvana breathed a sigh of relief. "Good."

"Shall we go in?" Lenad murmured. "Let these folk get on with their work."

"Oh, yes." Irvana nodded at the rest of the servants who bowed and curtsied as she passed. She was amused to see a flicker of unease on Alexia's face and paused in front of her. "I look forward to trying your pastry, Alexia. It always looked as though it would be delicious."

"Wha—! Oh, yes, veg gir—! My lady!" Alexia's cheeks turned red.

Irvana smiled. Maybe this homecoming wouldn't be as hard as she'd imagined.

She stepped through the main door and into the palace, her footsteps echoing on the white stone floor of the entrance hall. Thick columns, made of the same stone, held up a ceiling of coloured and frosted glass which patterned the white floor like a carpet. Between the columns were alcoves, each one home to a statue of sandy brown stone. She darted between the alcoves to take a closer look at the statues, and stopped in front of a carved lion.

If this was the entrance hall, how much grander were the other rooms? She'd only seen the kitchens and a couple of bedrooms when she was in her palace before.

Her palace.

Irvana couldn't help grinning.

"There should be enough time to hang the portrait before dinner, but what do you say to Graym taking you to your rooms first?" Lenad said.

Irvana turned away from the lion. "Graym? Not Sofan?"

Graym stepped forward and bowed his head. "I've been promoted, Lady Irvana. Until you find someone you'd rather have as your man. You might want a lady . . . There hasn't been a lady overlord for so long, no one's sure what you'll want."

Irvana looked at Lenad. "I can choose?"

Lenad nodded and tried to suppress a smile. "I'm sure you'll decide in time, but for now, Graym will do. I'll see you in the gallery when you've done, but for now, I'll leave you in Graym's capable hands."

Irvana could hardly contain herself. She wanted to run through the corridors, investigate all the rooms that were now hers. But there was no hurry; she had all the time in the world to explore her new home. Perhaps she could even stay here over the winter, make this her permanent residence.

"This way, my lady," Graym said.

She followed Graym along unfamiliar corridors until they reached a place she knew. How many times had she walked along this corridor, carrying the tray for Aymee? Graym opened a door and ushered Irvana into a room.

"Oh no!" Panic closed her throat, she felt faint. "I can't— not here!"

Graym frowned. "But this is the overlord's apartment. It's supposed to be yours."

Irvana took a deep breath. The desk was still there, the very same desk that Terenz had sat behind when he ordered her to hang. It was empty now of his papers and ink, but full of bad memories. Through an open door she glimpsed the bed he must have slept in and her stomach turned. There was still too much of him here, in the heavy wood panelling, the dark drapes and curtains . . .

"I'm sorry." She backed out of the room. "I can't. Please, isn't there somewhere else?"

Graym didn't look happy, but he closed the door on the memory of Terenz. He studied Irvana for a moment and gave a quick nod. "This way, my lady."

A little further down the corridor he showed her into another bedroom. "Will this do? Your grandmother, the Lady Beatrix, used this room while she lived."

Irvana's heart lifted. It was like walking into a room filled with sunshine. The wallpaper was covered in delicate yellow flowers, their blooms the same colour as the silk drapes and covers on the bed. The furniture was all made from a pale wood and a dark yellow rug covered the floor.

There was no trace of Terenz here.

"Graym, thank you. It's lovely. Have my trunks sent here, please. And let Rosann know where I am."

"Aye, my lady." Graym bowed and walked out of the bedroom. The door shut behind him with a little click.

Irvana threw herself backwards onto the four poster bed, arms spread wide. She was here at last. She'd had the golden star and the authority for months, but it hadn't felt real, until now . . .

"I'm the overlord of Koltarn," she whispered, and started to giggle.

A knock on the door made her sit up.

Rosann peeped in. "Irvana? Are you ready? Lenad's wondering where you are."

LENAD AND MIKAL were waiting in the portrait gallery.

"If the wind changes direction, your face'll stay like that," Lenad snapped.

Mikal scowled even more.

"I don't know what's got into you, but you had better get rid of it. And soon. I'll not have my page walking round with a face like thunder just because he didn't get to go to the fair."

"It's not that." Well, not entirely, Mikal's conscience forced him to add silently.

"Then what is it?"

Mikal shrugged. How could he explain that he'd dreaded coming back here? That that's why he'd been frowning at everyone and barely talking to them. Could they not see that for most of his life, Koltarn had been his summer home— his *home*? But Terenz's death had removed that privilege. He was only here now because Lenad was—and for the moment, remained—his master. To see so much that was familiar and know that none of it was his to enjoy like he had in the past . . .

Granted, he'd been allowed to use his old bedroom because it was near to Lenad and Faye's guest room, but the rest was off limits without permission. And the little worm of bitterness growing inside him could see only one person responsible for this—Irvana.

Lenad sighed. "Can you at least look happy when Irvana gets here and we unveil the portrait? I don't want anything—*anything*," his brows knitted together, "to spoil this moment for her. Understand?"

"Look happy? Why should I—?"

"I'm here!"

Mikal cut short his bitter reply and watched Irvana run towards them. He couldn't bear to see the happiness shining on her face.

"Right." Lenad rubbed his hands together. "Let's get this done, and we can all have dinner."

"It's so exciting. Don't you think so, Mikal?" Irvana's eyes were twinkling and her face was flushed.

Mikal grunted and hung back, allowing her to walk ahead with Lenad. As he passed under Terenz's portrait, he looked up, overcome with an urge to see his guardian's face again. But a sheet of black gauze obscured the features of The Black Star, and would continue to do so until the first anniversary of the overlord's death.

Lenad and Irvana stopped in front of a different frame— one covered with a white sheet.

"You are about to take your rightful place in the history of the StarMarks, Irvana," Lenad said.

He didn't want to see, but Mikal couldn't look away as Irvana tugged a corner of the cover. It came away easily, revealing the portrait underneath.

In the painting, Irvana was seated at a dressing table, looking into a mirror. Her reflection was smiling slightly, as though laughing at some secret joke. And perhaps she was. Her dark hair hung over her shoulder, revealing the golden star at the nape of her neck.

To Mikal, it felt like she was laughing directly at him. Bile rose up in his throat as the worm gnawed deeper into his gut. "Very nice," he muttered. "Got to go, things to do." He spun on his heel and walked away as fast as he could.

"Mikal? Mikal—wait!"

He heard Irvana's rapid footfalls behind him and quickened his pace. Irvana caught up and stepped in front of him, forcing him to stop. He gave her an impatient look.

What did she want now? Standing this close to her, he realised with a shock how much taller he'd grown. He was almost a man . . .

"Mikal, I wanted to tell you. Guess who I saw again in the market? Simean and Matild. They're coming to visit, you'll have to meet them—"

"Is that an order, my lady?" Mikal said.

"What?"

He ignored the hurt and confusion on her face. The worm had grown big and fat and was ready to bite back. "Is that an order? That I have to meet them?" Mikal fixed his gaze an inch above Irvana's head.

"No! I thought you'd like . . . I wanted you to . . . Mikal, what's wrong?"

"Nothing."

Irvana crossed her arms. "Are you still mad at me, because I went to the fair on my own? We can go again, tomorrow if you—"

"It's got nothing to do with the fair!" Mikal's voice was sharper than he'd intended. He caught Lenad frowning at him. "I wish I'd stayed in Bernea."

"Why? I thought you'd be glad to be back in Koltarn."

"Glad?" He was almost shouting now. "When I'm back in a place I used to have the run of but I'm now nothing but a servant? And when you've made it perfectly clear who's in charge here? I mean, you turned up late, kept everyone waiting for your grand entrance, and you never apologised."

"It wasn't like that—"

"You've thrown your weight around and demanded a new room because the overlord's apartments weren't good enough for you—"

"No, that's not what—" Irvana's cheeks flushed red.

"—the poor little orphan girl, pretending to be an overlord. Look at you! All dressed up and putting on airs and graces, revelling in everyone's admiration. And this!" He gestured at her portrait. "Getting us here to see your picture unveiled so we can tell you how good it looks and all the time, *all the time*, Terenz is hanging right beside it. Does it even matter to you that your uncle is dead? I suppose you'll order his portrait removed because he didn't have the all-important golden star like you and your father?"

"No! Mikal, stop!" Tears filled Irvana's eyes.

He turned away so he didn't have to see them. "I've not got to wait long before I'll inherit what's left of my father's estate and be out of your life. I'd hate to put a dampener on all the good times I've no doubt you're planning. It must be hell, having me under your nose all day, reminding you of Terenz." He'd said too much, lost control. Suddenly ashamed of himself, he bowed quickly. "I have duties. Excuse me, my lady."

He stepped past Irvana and walked away as fast as he could without breaking into an undignified run.

DINNER THAT EVENING was a quiet affair.

Merty had prepared a veritable banquet, but Irvana didn't feel much like eating. She pushed the food around her plate, her appetite all but gone after the confrontation with Mikal. His words had hurt—did he really think she was abusing her position already? He was jealous, that's all, she tried to tell herself. He hadn't appeared for the meal—though whether that was his own choice or a punishment inflicted by Lenad, she didn't know. And honestly, she didn't care. He'd not minced his words in the portrait gallery, and she didn't want another argument.

Perhaps she should have thought more about how he would feel, though, coming back to the palace.

Irvana had been devastated when she'd learnt of her uncle's death, in spite of all that he'd done. She'd hoped that, given time, Terenz would grow to like—even love—her, help her with the enormous task she faced. But it was not to be. She was alone. No family. Just a few friends to advise her . . . and it looked like she'd just lost one of them.

After dinner, in the library, Irvana trailed her fingers along the shelves of books. "Do you think Eran will arrive soon?" she asked Lenad, who was sitting in an easy chair and looking through a pile of paperwork.

"I'm sure he will not be far behind us."

Irvana leaned over the back of his chair. "What are you reading?"

"Maintenance reports for the palace," Lenad said, turning a page. "There is much to be done. Several of the bedrooms need redecorating after the roof was damaged during last winter's storms and began to leak. Repairs to the rotting pavilion on the cliff top have begun, and the stable renovations are close to completion. But there are many other minor things which need attention."

Irvana felt a rush of gratitude and placed a kiss on the top of Lenad's head. He looked up in surprise.

"Thank you," she said. "For looking after me and the palace while I'm still learning."

"It's my pleasure, my duty."

Irvana tried to stifle a huge yawn.

Lenad chuckled. "Looks like someone is ready for bed."

"It must be all the travelling. I think I'll get an early night." Irvana yawned again. "Goodnight."

CHAPTER 26
Fire!

A CLANGING BELL woke Mikal.

"What the—?"

He heard a distant shout.

"Fire!"

Fire? For one moment he was terrified into stillness, then he fought his sheets, tangling them round his arms and legs as he scrambled to get out of bed. Clothes—where were his clothes? A bitterness caught at the back of his throat as he snatched up his trousers and pulled them on—smoke. He flung the bedroom door open and heard shouts over the sound of the alarm bell. The corridor outside was hazy with swirling greyness.

"Mikal!" Lenad shouted from down the corridor.

"Here!"

Lenad appeared out of the smoke. His eyes were wild as he gripped Mikal's arm. "Get everybody out!"

"What are you—?"

But Lenad was already running away, his nightshirt flapping loosely above his trousers.

"Fire!" Mikal yelled. "Fire!"

He pounded on the door next to his own, his brain as foggy as the air in the corridor. How many people were sleeping down here?

Graym materialised out of the smoke. "Aymee's right down at the end!" He disappeared again.

A ghost floated towards Mikal. No—not a ghost—Faye, her hair loose about her shoulders. "Where's Irvana?"

Mikal's stomach clenched. The smoke was getting thicker,

wrapping itself around him like a bandage. "Haven't seen her. I—"

"Got her!"

"Irvana?" Mikal's relief was short lived. Graym appeared out of the smoke carrying Aymee, her arms wrapped tight around his neck.

"Let me help." Faye hurried forward to share Graym's load. "Mikal, find Irvana!"

He ran straight to the overlord's apartment and dashed inside. He darted into the bedroom and pulled up short, cursing his own stupidity. Irvana wasn't here, dammit! She'd chosen a different room—he'd known that! Precious moments ticked away until he found the right door.

"Irvana!" he yelled, thumping on the wood and rattling the handle. The door wouldn't open—she'd locked it. "Irvana! Open up!"

The back of his neck prickled at the sound of crackling above him. He glanced up—smoke was seeping through the ceiling.

He banged on the door again. "Irvana!"

Was that the rattle of a key in the lock? Yes!

He twisted the handle and pushed his way inside. "We have to go!"

Irvana backed away from him, moving deeper into the room instead of towards the door. Her eyes were huge in her pale face. "But the fire—"

He didn't have time for this. Mikal grabbed Irvana's hand and tugged her into the corridor.

The fire was not going to make it easy; thick black smoke billowed around them. Sparks filled the air, smouldering where they landed.

"We can't, it's too bad!" Irvana's voice rose with hysteria.

Mikal gritted his teeth. "We can and we will. Keep low."

He kept hold of Irvana and forced her to run behind him, aiming for the portrait gallery. Even doubled over, the flesh on the back of his neck felt as though it was blistering in the searing heat above his head, worse than any sunburn.

As they reached the end of the bedroom corridor, the ceiling behind them collapsed. Irvana screamed and fell to her knees.

"Get up!" Mikal wrenched her to her feet.

They had to keep going, find a way out before the fire caught up with them. Eyes watering, lungs burning, he pulled Irvana into the gallery. There was smoke, but no flame. In two strides, he was at the window, struggling with the catch. Irvana collapsed at his feet, coughing and choking. He tried to ignore her smudged face and the nightdress pocked with tiny burn marks.

"Open, damn you!"

Suddenly, the catch gave way. Sweet, clean air flooded over Mikal and he breathed deep, its coolness soothing his lungs as he pulled Irvana to her feet.

"Time to go." He pushed her outside and would have followed, but at that moment the curtains of heavy smoke parted. Standing a short distance away was a woman, cloaked and hooded, holding a lantern.

"Over here!" Mikal's voice was hoarse—was that why the woman didn't move? She hadn't heard him? Or was she too terrified? He leaned out of the window. "Go!" he shouted at Irvana. "Get away!"

He didn't wait to see where she was heading—it was enough to see that she started to run, and in the right direction; away from the burning building.

He turned back. The woman was invisible, shrouded in smoke so thick, he could have cut it with a knife. Burying his mouth and nose in the crook of his elbow, Mikal dived into the murk to find her.

She hadn't moved.

"Miss?" He coughed. "We have to go. Give me your—"

A gust of air from the open window blew the smoke aside for a second time and in the dim light of her lantern, he saw what held the woman's attention: the new portrait. Mikal glanced at it too and felt as though someone had punched him in the gut.

The canvas had been slashed to ribbons. Nothing was left. Irvana's smile, the golden star, her laughing eyes—all gone.

The woman finally looked at Mikal. Her face was streaked with soot. One eye was bruised and swollen shut, the other bright with excitement and fixed on him.

Icy fingers tiptoed down Mikal's spine. Recognition fought with disbelief. "Mistress Andela?"

"Hello, Mikal."

"Wha . . . what are you doing here?"

Andela gestured towards the portrait with her free hand. There was a flash of silver as the blade she was holding caught the lamplight. "Removing the opposition."

A knife. She had a knife—

"Terenz won't get his golden star otherwise."

Terenz? What was she talking about? Was she in shock? "B-but Terenz is dead," Mikal managed. "He'll never have a golden star."

"Dead?" Andela smiled and shook her head. "Of course he isn't. Who do you think did this?" She pointed to her eye. "He was angry that I'd not helped him sooner."

A giant vice closed around Mikal's chest. He couldn't breathe, and it had nothing to do with the smoke swirling around them both. "You're lying," he gasped. "Terenz is dead—I saw him die!"

There were cracks in the ceiling above him, cracks that glowed orange and hissed and spat flames. The fire had caught them.

"Why would I lie? Terenz is here, in Koltarn." Oblivious to the danger, Andela leaned closer, still smiling that odd smile. "He knows I love him, would do anything for him. That's why I agreed to help . . ." The knife fell from her hand as she patted at a smouldering patch on her cloak.

"You're mad!" Mikal backed away, coughing. The heat was unbearable now, scorching his lungs with every breath. A chunk of burning plaster fell at his feet. He had to get out.

"It was Terenz's idea, to flush Irvana out with fire," Andela continued, her voice thick and hoarse from the smoke. "With her gone, he wouldn't have to be the Black Star anymore."

With a roar, orange-white flames burst through the ceiling. Mikal dropped into a crouch and threw his arms over his head.

"I'll be the first to see his golden star!" Andela laughed at the fiery tongues reaching for her. She flung out her arms and began a slow pirouette, eyes unfocused and hair a mass of reflected fire.

Irvana was outside . . . and so was Terenz.

Terenz!

Mikal leapt through the open window with Andela's laughter ringing in his ears, hit the ground hard, and stumbled. Before he could scramble to his feet, a deafening explosion behind him made the ground tremble. The world turned orange and showered him with shards of broken glass.

Before the echo of Andela's scream had died away, Mikal was back on his feet and running into the darkness in the direction he thought Irvana had taken.

CHAPTER 27
The Darkest Hour

IRVANA RAN. LEGS pumping, heart pounding, aiming for somewhere safe. Just once, she glanced over her shoulder; flames were pouring out of the palace windows, licking at its roof, reaching up into the night sky and colouring the garden with orange and yellow. She stumbled and fell, but barely registered the damp grass under her cheek before she was up and running again, as though the fire was scorching her heels.

A thick hedge loomed out of the darkness, and she darted through a break in the leaves. It was quieter on the other side—no shouts or screams, no crackle of flame or shattering of glass. She was in the round garden, half of it in deep shadow beneath the towering hedge, the other half basking in bright moonlight.

Would she be safe here?

Irvana slowed to a walk, the crunch of gravel loud under her feet. She was drawn to the very centre of the garden, to the fountain, whose water had been turned to molten silver by the moon. She splashed water onto her face, gasping as the icy liquid made contact with her burning cheeks. Then she sat down with a thump on the fountain's base, her legs trembling and suddenly too weak to support her. She closed her eyes and leaned back against the damp stone, the chill seeping through her nightdress. She tried to block out the memory of the burning palace, but it was no use. All she could see in her mind's eye was fire.

Someone laughed.

She opened her eyes. Was she hearing things? No. A man had just limped out of the shadows into the moonlight. She pulled herself to her feet, trying to make out who it was. "Tolly? Is that you?"

The figure lurched closer. Not Tolly, even though he was limping like the old gatekeeper. Irvana frowned. This man was too tall, no sign of a crooked back. Who . . . ?

He stopped several paces away from her, his face concealed in the shadows of a hooded cloak. A hand, made pale by the moonlight, pushed the hood back as he spoke. "You're in my garden again, beet girl."

She froze, as if his voice had turned her to stone.

Terenz!

But Terenz, limping. Terenz, with a swathe of white hair growing through the black, glowing in the moonlight. Terenz, with half his face puckered and twisted almost beyond recognition. And his eyes . . . They were exactly the same as she remembered them. Steely grey and menacing, with rage flickering in their depths.

"How much change a year can bring," he murmured.

Was it really him? Or was she seeing a ghost? As Irvana's stomach heaved, she willed herself not to be sick, clutching at the fountain to keep herself upright.

"You died," she croaked. "They told me . . . the arrest . . ."

Terenz shook his head, grimacing as though the movement caused him pain. "Oh, I was closer to death then than I have ever been, but not near enough. And after? Others recognised my StarRing, delivered me eventually into the welcoming arms of Andela, who nursed me back to life. I thought I was her brother . . . that's what she told me. I was a broken man, you see. Could remember nothing. Disabled by my injuries, unable to remember my real name, but alive. And living here, in Koltarn."

He limped two steps closer.

"It all changed when I saw you at the fair, beet girl. I remembered it all—from overlord to cripple . . ." He chuckled—a mirthless, bitter sound.

"Yes, you were the overlord . . . I'm sorry," Irvana whispered. "I didn't mean for you to get hurt."

Terenz pressed the heel of his hand to his temple. "Is that so? Yet you signed the warrant, sent Lenad to arrest me—and look what happened."

Irvana flinched as he thrust his face forward. The moonlight showed his scars even more clearly—it looked as though his skin had melted, like candle wax. "It wasn't supposed to be like that. I just wanted to stop you fighting, was going to ask you to help me. You know so much about being an overlord—"

"Ha! So you'd have used my knowledge, my experience, to set yourself up?" Terenz shook his head. "I don't think so, beet girl." He almost spat the words at her. "I remembered what a good job I'd done, you see, decided I wanted the position back."

"But . . . you can't. I've got the golden star." Irvana touched the back of her neck, assuring herself that yes, it was still there.

"Andela told me." Terenz touched his cheek, where his own Mark was barely visible within the scarred flesh. "The thing is, I don't think that I need to worry about that."

Irvana blinked at him. "But—"

Terenz smiled. "You see, when my memory returned, I remembered the secret ways into these grounds and the layout of the palace. Knowing where to find the library was crucial for my fiery extravaganza. Andela was . . . persuaded . . . to help. All I had to do was wait for my long lost niece to show her face. And there you were, running straight into the arms of the Black Star!" He opened his arms wide, as though to embrace her.

"What?" Irvana couldn't make sense of what she was hearing. "I don't understand. *You* set fire to the palace? Why?"

"Because I'm going to kill you, beet girl."

Run! Instinct made Irvana flee before his words really registered. She veered left, then right, dodging and weaving along the intersecting gravel paths, fear driving her to put as much distance between herself and Terenz as she could.

"I may have a bad leg, but I'll catch up eventually, beet girl. I am going to reclaim my inheritance!" Terenz lurched after her, his uneven footsteps unexpectedly fast.

He mustn't catch her! Irvana dived into the shadows, aiming for a gateway in the hedge, but she misjudged the opening. Branches caught at her face and hands, snagged on her nightdress. She pulled herself free and carried on running towards the trees.

Even when clouds smothered the moon, plunging the garden into deep blackness, Irvana ran. She should have stopped. Without warning, her foot caught in something, sending her sprawling among a tangle of exposed roots, sharp pain knifing through her ankle. Blood pounded in her ears— she had to keep moving, couldn't stop. Terenz was coming . . .

Using the tree whose treacherous roots had tripped her for support, Irvana pulled herself up and tested the injured ankle. It bore her weight, but only just.

"Tired already? What a shame . . . I was having such fun . . ."

Terenz's velvety whisper was close. Too close.

A sob caught in Irvana's throat as she gritted her teeth against the pain and limped on.

"It appears we are more evenly matched in this chase. Both of us now have a leg that doesn't work."

He was getting closer.

The moon broke free from the cloud and lit up a building. Irvana sped towards it, her ankle on fire. She had to reach it, had to lock herself inside. She managed to climb the steps and almost fell through the doorway. She reached for the door to slam it shut—but there wasn't one. Nothing to bolt against Terenz—there weren't even any walls to speak of.

She heard Lenad's voice in her head. "Repairs . . . to the pavilion . . ." And look, there was a stack of planks and some tools on the floor.

With a jolt, Irvana realised where she was: the cliff top

pavilion. It was no more than a roof sitting on top of decorative pillars, which had walls that were only waist high. It might be the perfect building for enjoying scenic views over the sea, but it was useless in offering protection from a vengeful overlord. A giggle rose up in her throat, unexpected and inappropriate. She'd had the sudden and ridiculous idea of nailing the planks across the door to keep Terenz out.

"I always liked the view from here," Terenz said.

Irvana hesitated for the space of a heartbeat, then reached out and snatched up a hammer. She wheeled round to face her uncle, the makeshift weapon gripped tightly behind her back.

Terenz hauled his crippled leg up every step. When he reached the top, he smiled. In the moonlight his teeth flashed white, the StarMark a fragmented and distorted shadow on his cheek.

"I shall come here every day after I am reinstated," he said, gazing out over a sea flecked with silver-edged waves. Suddenly he groaned and bent almost double, hands pressed either side of his head.

Irvana tried to control the dry sobs which shook her body. She would need all her breath for what she was planning.

Whatever afflicted Terenz passed—he straightened and turned towards her. "I think we have reached the end, don't you?" A slow grin twisted his already disfigured features into a hideous mask. "How tragic that in the dark, terrified by the fire and utterly alone, you lost your way in the garden and plunged to your death."

"No, please . . . please don't . . ." Irvana begged.

Terenz lunged at her, hands reaching for her throat.

Irvana screamed. With every ounce of the strength she had left, she swung the hammer.

Terenz cursed as it whistled past his ear. Before she could strike again, he caught Irvana's arm, wrenched the hammer from her grip and flung it away, over the sea.

Irvana screamed again and somewhere in the distance was an answering shout.

"You think someone will save you?" Terenz snarled, pulling her close. "You'll be dead before they get here." He towered over her, his breath warm on her skin, eyes riveted on her face as though he would imprint her features onto his memory. "I am going to squeeze the life from you, beet girl," he whispered.

"No!" Irvana fought then like a thing possessed, screaming and scratching at Terenz's face with her free hand, trying to break free. He was too strong, there was no escaping him. The fight went out of her, melted right away, and Irvana sagged in his arms. A deadly lethargy had taken her over—her limbs would not respond and her voice had been silenced.

The StarRing on Terenz's finger reflected the moon in a flash of pure silver as he stroked Irvana's cheek. "It will soon be over," he told her, as his fingers closed around her throat.

The pressure increased. The shadows at the edge of Irvana's vision deepened until she was peering down a glittering tunnel, drowning in Terenz's gaze, her mind filled with unending blackness and eternal silence.

But then the silence was broken by a sound of raw anguish, of unendurable pain, and the pressure on Irvana's throat disappeared.

She could breathe!

Irvana collapsed to her hands and knees, sucking in great lungfuls of air to ease the pain in her chest. Through streaming eyes, she looked up. The Black Star was moaning and thumping the side of his head. With a roar, he clutched a fistful of his own hair and pulled a great clump of black and white strands loose.

"Uncle!" She couldn't bear to see his pain.

"Irvana?" Terenz shook his head as though to clear it. "Where are you?" He staggered sideways, catching his foot on the pile of planks. He fell against the low wall of the pavilion.

With a crack, the rotten wood split under his weight. The decayed planks fell away, following the hammer over the edge of the cliff.

Terenz flung out a hand, caught hold of an upright pillar to stop himself falling. His expression of relief turned to one of horror as the wood crumbled under his hand. His long fingers tore desperately at the wood, seeking a purchase, but it was too late—there was nothing of substance left to hold. His arms windmilled wildly as he overbalanced.

"No!" Irvana reached out, tried to catch him.

The cloth of his trousers skimmed past her hand, light as the wings of a butterfly. Then Terenz was gone. He screamed once, a thin, terrified sound. It ended abruptly in a sickening thud.

"No! Oh, no!"

Irvana dragged herself to the hole in the wall where Terenz had disappeared. Slowly, she inched forward. The sheer cliff dropped away beneath her, making her head spin. Far, far below, there was something—a broken doll?—lying on the rocks. A pool of something dark formed a halo around its head.

"Terenz," she whispered, and the doll's outline blurred. She had to get back to the palace, tell them what had happened. Get help . . . Tears ran freely down her cheeks as she reached for the nearest upright to pull herself up. She snatched her hand away. What if this post was as rotten as the one Terenz had grabbed? Sent her crashing after him? No—she would not trust any part of the structure now. She pushed herself to her feet, and limped across to the doorway.

"Irvana!"

Someone was sprinting across the grass towards her.

Irvana wiped her eyes, trying to see who it was. "Mikal!"

He leapt up the steps, and she raised a hand to stop him. "Careful," she gasped. "The pavilion's not safe."

"Never mind that. Terenz is here, somewhere." Mikal's face was black with soot, his hair singed at the ends.

"I know."

"You've seen him?"

All she could do was point towards the ragged hole in the side of the pavilion.

"What do you—?" Understanding dawned on Mikal's face. "He fell?"

It took a huge effort to nod. The terror which had been driving Irvana drained away. She was so tired now, so weak. Her head was thumping, her throat was raw, and there was an old ache in her chest.

Mikal's face blurred in front of her. "Irvana?" he said, from a long, long distance away.

With a sigh, Irvana gave herself up to the blackness that seemed so eager to swallow her . . .

CHAPTER 28
A Brighter Star

THERE WAS STILL some scaffolding around the palace a year after the fire.

The gardeners had done their best, filling the gardens with colour, but the smoke-blackened walls and new roof were reminders of the disaster they were trying to hide.

As soon as the fire had been brought under control, leaving most of the palace a blackened shell, Irvana had been whisked away to Bernea until it became clear that Terenz and Andela had acted alone and there was no further risk to her life.

She still had nightmares about that night. She would wake in a panic, struggling to breathe and fighting bedcovers which, in her dream, had become the arms of her uncle. Koltarn had had to do without its overlord for another twelve months while she recovered from the trauma.

Yet in recent weeks, Irvana had found herself wanting to return.

"The palace isn't completely finished," Lenad warned her. "There are still workmen present."

"I don't care," Irvana said. "I want to go home."

And now she was here, all she wanted to do was get away. She'd been excited to see how the new palace was shaping up, but hadn't bargained on meeting ghosts there, who forced her to remember things she'd rather forget.

Two of the ghosts had been laid to rest on the cliff top.

Irvana found herself in the grounds, walking the path towards their grave. On the way, she broke two or three stems from a rose bush and buried her nose in the flowers. They were so darkly red, they were almost black.

She reached the grave and found someone was already there. A man, standing beside the obelisk of black onyx carved with a seven pointed star. He looked familiar.

"Mikal?"

At first she wasn't sure it *was* him, even when he turned round. He'd changed so much since she last saw him. When had that been? Last autumn, when he left Lenad's service—finally of an age to manage the estate he'd inherited from his father. How tall he was, how broad his chest. Mikal didn't look much like a boy any more. Irvana felt suddenly shy in his presence.

"Forgive me, my lady," Mikal said, bowing. "I came to pay my respects. I didn't think you'd mind."

Irvana noticed he didn't meet her eye. "I don't. It's good to see you, Mikal." She took a step closer to him. "Why don't you ever come to see us?"

He shrugged. "I have my own place now, need to manage it. I don't have a lot of spare time."

"Lenad misses you." I miss you, Irvana thought, but she didn't say it.

"He shouldn't." Mikal flicked a glance at Irvana and looked away again. "I wasn't a very good page."

An uncomfortable silence fell between them then, broken only by the sound of the sea crashing against the rocks hundreds of feet below.

"You brought flowers?" Mikal said, pointing to Irvana's hands.

"Flowers?" Irvana looked down—she'd forgotten the roses she held in the surprise of seeing him. "Yes . . ." She stepped around Mikal and laid the flowers at the base of the obelisk. Poor Terenz. And poor Andela. They'd both wanted something they could not have—and look where it had landed them. It had taken a while before Irvana had allowed herself to believe that she was not responsible for their deaths—Terenz and Andela had been faced with a choice and made the wrong one. Yet she still felt guilty, as guilty as she felt about Niklos or Davith. If she'd never left the shack, never come to Koltarn, perhaps they'd all still be alive . . .

"Did you push him?"

"What?" Irvana spun round.

"Did you push him?" Mikal was definitely looking at her now—staring intently in fact. "I can't help wondering whether what happened to Terenz really was an accident."

"I didn't push him." Irvana forced the words out, past the bands of guilt that had tightened around her throat as in her mind's eye she saw a man falling from the cliff edge. Mikal had thought her capable of making that happen? No wonder he'd kept his distance from her for so long. "He fell. I wish he hadn't."

"Huh." Mikal nodded. "You know, I hated you when Terenz died."

Irvana fell back against the obelisk as though Mikal had actually struck her. She'd thought he was her friend—yet he hated her. Her hand shot to her mouth, stifling a cry of disbelief.

"It was you that made him so damn stubborn about the Mark and what he was going to lose. Perhaps, if he'd been more flexible instead, accepted the way things turned out, he'd still be here, helping you to be Koltarn's overlord." Mikal sighed. "Instead, he died trying to kill you. Yes, I hated you for that."

She had to ask, but she was afraid of the answer. "Do you still hate me?"

"Of course not." Mikal looked genuinely shocked. "It was easy to blame someone else—you—for his death, yet I knew it wasn't your fault really. That's when I started to hate myself." He shuffled his feet. "Terenz had rubbed off on me more than I realised. I kept my distance because I didn't want to hurt you anymore."

"Oh, Mikal!" Irvana grabbed both of Mikal's hands and gripped them tight, forcing him to look at her. "You're nothing like Terenz. The first time I met you, you made me laugh. When you found the StarRing, you took it straight to Niklos and because of that, we found out the truth of who I was. You helped me to escape to Bernea and stood up to Davith when he chose Terenz over me. You have never acted like Terenz. You were—still are—my friend."

Mikal gently disentangled his hands. "But you lost so much because of him."

Irvana tried to laugh. "What did I lose? About half of a palace that was far too draughty to live in over the winter and a few portraits."

It had taken a long while to come to terms with the loss of her father's portrait. The only thing that remained of him now was his banner in Bernea, hanging alongside that of his brother. Even the locket had perished in the fire, melted shut from the heat.

"It's not all bad," she continued. "The palace is being redesigned—that's why the work's taking so long. I've decided to make Koltarn my permanent home and the new building needs to be more suitable for colder weather. I don't want to freeze in the winter. And of course, I need enough guest rooms for friends like you to visit."

"Really? After everything that happened, you'd still consider me a friend?" Mikal shook his head. "I don't deserve that."

"None of us deserve anything," Irvana said. "We don't deserve bad things happening to us, but they do. We probably don't deserve good things either, but when they happen, we enjoy them. I'd very much like you to enjoy being my friend."

He smiled at that. The familiar twinkle appeared in his eye. "Then I shall."

Irvana grinned. "I ought to be getting back. I've got a lot of unpacking to do. That's really why I snuck out. Rosann will do a much better job than me, but I bet she's really mad by now because she's doing it on her own." She held out a hand. "Come with me? Maybe when she sees you, she'll forget how cross she is? And I'm sure Lenad would like to hear how his old page is getting on in the world."

Mikal took her hand. "I'll come, my lady."

She slapped him lightly. "None of that. I'll always be your Irvana." What had she just said? *Your* Irvana? Heat crept across her cheeks and she dropped her eyes.

"My Irvana." Mikal chuckled. "I like that."

Peeping at him from under her lashes, Irvana thought that he looked very pleased with himself. "But, of course, the same goes for Lenad and Faye and Rosann. I'm their Irvana too."

Of course she was, but not in quite the same way—and both of them knew it.

Taking her by surprise, Mikal planted a swift kiss on her cheek. "Let's go."

That's when Irvana saw it—the future unfolding before her. A destiny which included Koltarn and an awful lot of Mikal.

"Race you!" she shouted and she was off and running towards the palace, leaving behind her the shadow of the Black Star for a future that was rather more golden.

Katherine Hetzel has always loved the written word, but only started writing "properly" after giving up her job as a pharmaceutical microbiologist to be a stay-at-home mum. The silly songs and daft poems she wrote for her children grew into longer stories. They ended up on paper and then published. (*Granny Rainbow*, Panda Eyes, 2014, *More Granny Rainbow*, Panda Eyes, 2015) She sees herself first and foremost as a children's author, passionate about getting kids reading, but she also enjoys writing short stories for adults and has been published in several anthologies. A member of the online writing community The Word Cloud, Katherine operates under the name of Squidge and blogs at Squidge's Scribbles. She lives in the heart of the UK with Mr Squidge and two teenaged children.